Caroline Snowden Guild

Hymns for Mothers and Children

SALZWASSER
VERLAG

Caroline Snowden Guild

Hymns for Mothers and Children

Reprint of the original, first published in 1861.

1st Edition 2022 | ISBN: 978-3-37505-793-0

Verlag (Publisher): Salzwasser Verlag GmbH, Zeilweg 44, 60439 Frankfurt, Deutschland
Vertretungsberechtigt (Authorized to represent): E. Roepke, Zeilweg 44, 60439 Frankfurt, Deutschland
Druck (Print): Books on Demand GmbH, In de Tarpen 42, 22848 Norderstedt, Deutschland

HYMNS

FOR

MOTHERS AND CHILDREN.

COMPILED BY

THE AUTHOR OF "VIOLET," "DAISY," &c.

BOSTON:

WALKER, WISE, AND COMPANY,

245 WASHINGTON STREET.

1861.

PREFACE.

SINCE the publication of the Hymns of the Ages, its compilers have frequently been urged to prepare a volume of like character for children.

One of them has accordingly given the leisure of several years to the present work; her plan being, to collect devout, entertaining, and suggestive poetry, — morning and evening hymns, and those calculated to stimulate the imagination, refine the taste, and train the child's heart to become strong, humane, and brave, as well as keep it gentle, reverent, and pure.

Finding a sad lack of material, she offers the volume now with diffidence, hoping that at least its deficiencies may draw some true poet's attention to the wants of "these little ones," that they may no longer be offered thin and coarse dilutions of morality, but hymns delicate, beautiful, and rare, as the souls which wait to receive them.

Meantime, such as her work is, she would cordially thank the many mothers who have encouraged and assisted in its preparation, and the many little Lilies, Freddies, and Kitties who have lent their favorite volumes for inspection, and oft-times taught the merit of the hymns by their loving and tender recital; — for there are no Athenæum libraries of children's books, and this has literally been gathered " out of the mouth of babes."

C. S. W.

Roxbury, October 16, 1860.

CONTENTS.

PART I.

CHILDREN.

PART II.

FOR YOUNG CHILDREN.

vi CONTENTS.

PART III.

NATURE.

PART IV.

RELIGIOUS INSTRUCTION.

I. THE HEAVENLY FATHER.

II. THE GOOD SHEPHERD.

III. MORNING AND EVENING HYMNS.

IV. MISCELLANEOUS.

PART V.

OLDER CHILDREN.

PART VI.

THE END.

PART I.

CHILDREN.

THE BABY.

ANOTHER little wave
   Upon the sea of life;
Another soul to save
   Amid its toil and strife.

Two more little feet
　　To walk the dusty road ;
To choose where two paths meet,
　　The narrow and the broad.

Two more little hands
　　To work for good or ill ;
Two more little eyes,
　　Another little will.

Another heart to love,
　　Receiving love again ;
And so the baby came,
　　A thing of joy and pain.

Providence Journal.

MY BABY.

Cheeks as soft as July peaches, —
Lips whose velvet scarlet teaches
Poppies paleness, — round, large eyes,
Ever great with new surprise, —
Minutes filled with shadeless gladness, —
Minutes just as brimmed with sadness, —
Happy smiles and wailing cries,
Crows and laughs and tearful eyes,
Lights and shadows, swifter born
Than on wind-swept autumn corn,

Ever some new tiny notion,
Making every limb all motion,
Catchings up of legs and arms,
Throwings back and small alarms,
Clutching fingers, — straitening jerks,
Twining feet whose each toe works,
Kickings up and straining risings,
Mother's ever-new surprisings,
Hands all wants and looks all wonder
At all things the heavens under,
Tiny scorns of smiled reprovings
That have more of love than lovings,
Mischiefs done with such a winning
Archness that we prize such sinning;
Breakings dire of plates and glasses,
Graspings small at all that passes;
Pullings off of all that 's able
To be caught from tray or table;
Silences, — small meditations,
Deep as thoughts of cares for nations,
Breaking into wisest speeches
In a tongue that nothing teaches,
All the thoughts of whose possessing
Must be wooed to light by guessing;
Slumbers, — such sweet angel-seemings
That we 'd ever have such dreamings,
Till from sleep we see thee breaking,
And we 'd always have thee waking;
Wealth for which we know no measure,
Pleasure high above all pleasure,

Gladness brimming over gladness,
Joy in care, — delight in sadness,
Loveliness beyond completeness,
Sweetness distancing all sweetness,
Beauty all that beauty may be,
That's May Bennett, — that's my baby.

W. C. BENNETT.

THE BABIE.

NAE shoon to hide her tiny tae,
　Nae stocking on her feet ;
Her supple ankles white as snaw,
　Or early blossoms sweet.

Her simple dress of sprinkled pink,
　Her double dimpled chin,
Her puckered lip and baumy mow,
　With na one tooth between.

Her een, sae like her mither's een,
　Two gentle liquid things ;
Her face is like an angel's face, —
　We 're glad she has no wings.

She is the budding o' our love
　A giftie God gie'd us ;
We munna luve the gift ow'r weel,
　'T wad be nae blessing thus.

A CRADLE SONG.

Soft be the hour of thy sleeping,
  Little one mine, dear little one mine ;
Safe, gentle lamb, be thy keeping,
  In the arms of the Shepherd divine ;
    Fond as thy mother's love,
    Yet there is One above
      Loves thee still dearer,
    And — when for thee she prays ·
    Grace, peace, and happy days —
      Bends down to hear her.

Glad be the hour of thy waking,
  Little one mine, dear little one mine,
God grant that the pangs of heart-breaking
  Never visit that bosom of thine.
    God grant thy stream of life,
    Unvexed by guilt and strife,
      Gently may flow ;
    And when the time shall come,
    To thy eternal home
      'T is thine to go,
Calm be the hour of thy dying,
Loved one of mine, dear loved one of mine ;
Untrammelled thy spirit, when flying
To the land where the holy ones shine.

                              REV. W. CALVERT.

CRADLE SONG.

SLEEP, baby, sleep!
Thy father watches the sheep,
Thy mother is shaking the dream-land tree,
And down falls a little dream on thee;
Sleep, baby, sleep!

Sleep, baby, sleep!
The large stars are the sheep,
The little stars are the lambs, I guess,
The fair moon is the shepherdess;
Sleep, baby, sleep!

Sleep, baby, sleep!
Our Saviour loves his sheep;
He is the Lamb of God on high,
Who for our sakes came down to die.
Sleep, baby, sleep!

Sleep, baby, sleep!
I'll buy for thee a sheep,
With a golden bell so fine to see,
And it shall frisk and play with thee,
Sleep, baby, sleep!

Sleep, baby, sleep!
And cry not like a sheep;

Else will the sheep-dog bark and whine,
And bite this naughty child of mine.
    Sleep, baby, sleep!

    Sleep, baby, sleep!
    Away! and tend the sheep.
Away, thou black dog, fierce and wild,
And do not wake my little child!
    Sleep, baby, sleep!

SONG FROM THE GERMAN.

LULLABY.

LULLABY! O lullaby!
Baby, hush that little cry!
    Light is dying,
    Bats are flying —
Bees to-day with work have done;
So, till comes the morrow's sun,
Let sleep kiss those bright eyes dry!
    Lullaby! O lullaby!

Lullaby! O lullaby!
Hushed are all things far and nigh;
    Flowers are closing,
    Birds reposing,
All sweet things with life have done.
Sweet, till dawns the morning sun,
Sleep then kiss those blue eyes dry!
    Lullaby! O lullaby!

WM. C. BENNETT.

A ROCKING HYMN.

SWEET baby, sleep; what ails my dear;
What ails my darling thus to cry?
Be still, my child, and lend thine ear,
To hear me sing thy lullaby.
    My pretty lamb, forbear to weep;
    Be still, my dear; sweet baby, sleep.

Thou blessed soul, what canst thou fear?
What thing to thee can mischief do?
Thy God is now thy Father dear,
His holy Church thy mother too.
    Sweet baby, then forbear to weep;
    Be still, my babe; sweet baby, sleep.

Whilst thus thy lullaby I sing,
For thee great blessings ripening be;
Thine eldest brother is a King,
And hath a kingdom bought for thee.
    Sweet baby, then forbear to weep;
    Be still my babe; sweet baby, sleep.

Sweet baby, sleep, and nothing fear,
For whosoever thee offends,
By thy Protector threatened are,
And God! and angels are thy friends.
    Sweet baby, then forbear to weep;
    Be still, my babe; sweet baby, sleep.

GEORGE WITHER.

THE LITTLE ONES IN BED.

A ROW of little faces in the bed;
A row of little hands upon the spread;
A row of little roguish eyes all closed;
A row of little naked feet exposed.

A gentle mother leads them in their praise,
Teaching their feet to tread in heavenly ways,
And takes this lull in childhood's tiny tide,
The little errors of the day to chide.

Then tumbling headlong into waiting beds,
Beneath the sheets they hide their timid heads;
Till slumber steals away their idle fears,
And like a peeping bud each face appears.

All dressed like angels in their gowns of white,
They ' ~~fted to the skies in dreams of night;
And ʌraven . . . sparkle in their eyes at morn,
And stolen graces all their ways adorn.

THE PATTER OF LITTLE FEET.

UP with the sun in the morning,
  Away to the garden he hies,
To see if the sleepy blossoms
  Have begun to open their eyes.

Running a race with the wind,
  With a step as light and fleet,
Under my window I hear
  The patter of little feet.

Now to the brook he wanders
  In swift and noiseless flight,
Splashing the sparkling ripples
  Like a fairy water-sprite.
No sand under fabled river
  Has gleams like his golden hair,
No pearly sea-shell is fairer
  Than his slender ankles bare ;
Nor the rosiest stem of coral
  That blushes in ocean's bed
Is sweet as the flush that follows
  Our darling's airy tread.

From a broad window my neighbor
  Looks down on our little cot,
And watches the " poor man's blessing " —
  I cannot envy his lot.
He has pictures, books, and music,
  Bright fountains, and noble trees,
Flowers that blossom in roses,
  Birds from beyond the seas ;
But never does childish laughter
  His homeward footsteps greet,
His stately halls ne'er echo
  To the tread of innocent feet.

This child is our " speaking picture,"
  A birdling that chatters and sings,
Sometimes a sleeping cherub —
  (Our other one has wings,)
His heart is a charmed casket,
  Full of all that 's cunning and sweet,
And no harp-strings hold such music
  As follows his twinkling feet.

When the glory of sunset opens
  The highway by angels trod,
And seems to unbar the city
  Whose builder and maker is God,
Close to the crystal portal,
  I see by the gates of pearl,
The eyes of our other angel. —
  A twin-born little girl.

And I ask to be taught and directed
  To guide his footsteps aright,
So that I be accounted worthy
  To walk in sandals of light,
And hear amid songs of welcome
  From messengers trusty and fleet,
On the starry floor of heaven,
  The patter of little feet.

TO MY GODCHILD, ALICE.

ALICE, Alice, little Alice
My new christened baby Alice,
  Can there ever rhymes be found
To express my wishes for thee
In a silvery flowing, worthy
  Of that silver sound?
Bonnie Alice, Lady Alice,
  Sure, this sweetest name must be
A true omen to thee, Alice,
  Of a life's long melody.

Alice, Alice, little Alice,
May'st thou prove a golden chalice,
  Filled with holiness like wine;
With rich blessings running o'er,
Yet replenished evermore
  From a fount Divine:
Alice, Alice, little Alice,
  When this future comes to thee,
In thy young life's brimming chalice
  Keep some drops of balm for me!

Alice, Alice, little Alice,
Mayst thou grow a goodly palace,
  Fitly framed from roof to floors,
Pure unto the inmost centre,
While high thoughts like angels enter

At the open doors:
Alice, Alice, little Alice,
　　When this beauteous sight I see,
In thy woman-heart's wide palace
　　Keep one nook of love for me.

Alice, Alice, little Alice, —
Sure the verse halts out of malice
　　To the thoughts it feebly bears,
And thy name's soft echoes, ranging
From quaint rhyme to rhyme, are changing
　　Into silent prayers.
God be with thee, little Alice,
　　Of His bounteousness may He
Fill the chalice, build the palace,
　　Here, unto eternity!

Miss Muloch.

PEASANT CHILDREN.

Everywhere, everywhere,
　　Like the butterfly's silver wings,
That are seen by all in the summer air,
　　We meet with these beautiful things!
And the low, sweet lisp of the baby child
　　By a thousand hills is heard,
And the voice of the young heart's laughter, wild
　　As the voice of a singing bird!

The cradle rocks in the peasant's cot,
　As it rocks in the noble's hall,
And the brightest gift in the loftiest lot
　Is a gift that is given to all;
For the sunny light of childhood's eyes
　Is a boon like the common air,
And like the sunshine of the skies,
　It falleth everywhere!

They tell us that old Earth no more
　By angel feet is trod,
They bring not now as they brought of yore
　The oracles of God.
O, each of these young human flowers
　God's own high message bears,
And we are walking all our hours
　With "angels unawares"!

By stifling street and breezy hill
　We meet their spirit mirth;
That such bright shapes should linger till
　They take the stains of earth!
O, play not those a blessed part
　To whom the boon is given
To leave their errand with the heart,
　And straight return to heaven!

MARY HOWITT.

THE CHILDREN'S PRAYER.

BEAUTIFUL the children's faces!
  Spite of all that mars and sears:
To my inmost heart appealing;
Calling forth love's tenderest feeling:
  Steeping all my soul with tears.

Eloquent the children's faces —
  Poverty's lean look, which saith,
Save us! save us! woe surrounds us;
Little knowledge sore confounds us;
  Life is but a lingering death.

Give us light amid our darkness;
  Let us know the good from ill;
Hate us not for all our blindness;
Love us, lead us, show us kindness,
  You can make us what you will.

We are willing; we are ready;
  We would learn if you would teach;
We have hearts that yearn towards duty;
We have minds alive to beauty;
  Souls that any height can reach.

Raise us by your Christian knowledge:
  Consecrate to man our powers;
Let us take our proper station;

2

We, the rising generation,
 Let us stamp the age as ours.

We shall be what you will make us ; —
 Make us wise, and make us good :
Make us strong in time of trial ;
Teach us temperance, self-denial,
 Patience, kindness, fortitude !

Look into our childish faces ;
 See ye not our willing hearts ?
Only love us, — only lead us ;
Only let us know you need us,
 And we all will do our parts.

We are thousands — many thousands !
 Every day our ranks increase ;
Let us march beneath your banner,
We, the legion of true honor,
 Combating for love and peace !

Train us ! try us ! days slide onward,
 They can ne'er be ours again :
Save us, save ! from our undoing !
Save from ignorance and ruin ;
 Make us worthy to be MEN !

Send us to our weeping mothers,
 Angel-stamped in heart and brow ;
We may be our father's teachers :

We may be the mightiest preachers,
  In the day that dawneth now!

Such the children's mute appealing!
  All my inmost soul was stirred;
And my heart was bowed with sadness,
When a cry, like summer's gladness,
  Said, " The children's prayer is heard ! "
MARY HOWITT.

MY LITTLE DAUGHTER'S SHOES.

Two little rough, worn, stubbed shoes,
  A plump, well-trodden pair,
With striped stockings thrust within,
  Lie just beside my chair.

Of very homely fabric they,
  A hole is in each toe,
They might have cost, when they were new,
  Some fifty cents or so.

And yet this little worn-out pair
  Is richer far to me,
Than all the jewelled sandals are
  Of Eastern luxury.

This mottled leather, cracked with use,
  Is satin in my sight,

These little tarnished buttons shine
   With all a diamond's light.

Search through the wardrobe of the world !
   You shall not find me there
So rarely made, so richly wrought,
   So glorious a pair.

And why ?   Because they tell of her,
   Now sound asleep above,
Whose form is moving beauty, and
   Whose heart is beating love.

They tell me of her merry laugh,
   Her rich, whole-hearted glee ;
Her gentleness, her innocence,
   And infant purity.

They tell me that her wavering steps
   Will long demand my aid ;
For the old road of human life
   Is very roughly laid.

High hills and swift descents abound,
   And, on so rude a way,
Feet that can wear these coverings
   Would surely go astray.

Sweet little girl ! be mine the task
   Thy feeble steps to tend !

To be thy guide, thy counsellor,
  Thy playmate, and thy friend!

And when my steps shall faltering grow,
  And thine be firm and strong,
Thy strength shall lead my tottering age
  In cheerful peace along!

C. J. SPRAGUE.

BABY'S SHOES.

O THOSE little, those little blue shoes!
Those shoes that no little feet use!
    O the price were high
    That those shoes would buy,
Those little blue unused shoes!

For they hold the small shape of feet
That no more their mother's eyes meet,
    That, by God's good will,
    Years since grew still,
And ceased from their totter so sweet!

And O, since that baby slept,
So hushed! how the mother has kept,
    With a tearful pleasure,
    That little dear treasure,
And o'er them thought and wept!

For they mind her forevermore
Of a patter along the floor,
    And blue eyes she sees
    Look up from her knees,
With the look that in life they wore.

As they lie before her there,
There babbles from chair to chair,
    A little sweet face
    That's a gleam in the place,
With its little gold curls of hair.

Then O, wonder not that her heart
From all else would rather part
    Than those tiny blue shoes
    That no little feet use,
And whose sight makes such fond tears start.

W. C. BENNETT.

AN ANGEL IN THE HOUSE.

How sweet it were, if without feeble fright,
Or dying of the dreadful beauteous sight,
An angel came to us, and we could bear
To see him issue from the silent air
At evening in our room, and bend on ours
His divine eyes, and bring us from his bowers
News of dear friends and children who have never
Been dead indeed, — as we shall know forever.

Alas! we think not what we daily see
About our hearths, — angels, that *are* to be,
Or may be if they will, and we prepare
Their souls and ours to meet in happy air, —
A child, a friend, a wife whose soft heart sings
In unison with ours, breathing its future wings.

LEIGH HUNT.

PART II.

FOR YOUNG CHILDREN.

CREEP BEFORE YOU WALK.

FROM "WILLIE WINKIE."

CREEP away, my bairnie,
Creep before you gang,
Listen with both ears
To your old Granny's sang;
If you go as far as I,
You will think the road lang,
Creep away, my bairnie,
Creep before you gang.

Creep away, my bairnie,
Your're too young to learn
To tot up and down yet,
My bonnie wee bairn ;
Better creeping, careful,
Than falling with a bang,
Hurting all your wee brow, —
Creep before you gang.

The little birdie falls
When it tries too soon to fly,
Folks are sure to tumble
When they climb too high ;
Those who do not walk aright
Are sure to come to wrang, —
Creep away, my bairnie,
Creep before you gang.

JAMES BALLANTYNE.

THE TURTLE-DOVES.

VERY high in the pine-tree
The little Turtle-dove
Made a pretty little nursery,
To please her little love.
She was gentle, she was soft,
And her large dark eye

Often turned to her mate,
　Who was sitting close by.

" Coo," said the Turtle-dove,
　" Coo," said she,
" O, I love thee," said the Turtle-dove,
　" And I love THEE."
In the long, shady branches
　Of the dark pine-tree,
How happy were the doves,
　In their little nursery.

The young turtle-doves
　Never quarrelled in the nest;
For they dearly loved each other,
　Though they loved their mother best.
" Coo," said the little doves,
　" Coo," said she,
And they played together kindly,
　In the dark pine-tree.

Is this nursery of yours,
　Little sister, little brother,
Like the Turtle-doves' nest, —
　Do you love one another?
Are you kind, are you gentle,
　As children ought to be?
Then the happiest of nests
　Is your own nursery.

AUNT EFFIE'S RHYMES.

WHAT A CHILD HAS.

THE snail, see, has a house ;
A fur coat has the mouse ;
The sparrow has its feathers brown ;
The butterfly its wings of down.

Now tell me, darling, what have you ?
" I have clothes, and on each foot a shoe ;
Father and mother, life and glee ;
So good has God been unto me."

SONGS FROM THE GERMAN

WHAT I LOVE.

I LOVE my mother's gentle kiss,
    I love to join my brother's play,
I love to walk with little sis,
    And view the shops and pictures gay.

I love my toys and books to see,
    I love god-mother's silver cup,
But the best thing of things to me,
    Is when my father takes me up.

Father, when I 'm as tall as you,
    And you are small like little sis,
I 'll lay you on my shoulder too,
    And let you feel how nice it is.

MRS. GILMAN.

THE LITTLE ANGEL.

RIGHT into our house one day,
  A dear little angel came ;
I ran to him, and said softly,
  " Little angel, what is your name ? "

He said not a word in answer,
  But smiled a beautiful smile,
Then I said : " May I go home with you ?
  Shall you go in a little while ? "

But mamma said : " Dear little angel,
  Don't leave us ! O, always stay !
We will all of us love you dearly !
  Sweet angel ! O, don't go away ! "

So he stayed, and he stayed, and we loved him,
  As we could not have loved another ;
Do you want to know what his name is ?
  His name is — *my little brother !*

MELODIES FOR CHILDHOOD.

LITTLE RAIN-DROPS.

O WHERE do you come from,
  You little drops of rain,

Pitter patter, pitter patter,
   Down the window pane ?

They won't let me walk,
   And they won't let me play,
And they won't let me go
   Out of doors at all to-day.

They put away my playthings,
   Because I broke them all ;
And then they locked up all my bricks,
   And took away my ball.

Tell me, little rain-drops,
   Is that the way you play, —
Pitter patter, pitter patter, —
   All the rainy day ?

They say I 'm very naughty :
   But I 've nothing else to do
But sit here at the window ;
   I should like to play with you.

The little rain-drops cannot speak :
   But pitter-patter-pat
Means, " We can play on *this* side,
   Why can't you play on *that ?* "

AUNT EFFIE'S RHYMES.

THE DARLING LITTLE GIRL.

WHO 's the darling little girl
    Everybody loves to see ?
She it is whose sunny face
    Is as sweet as sweet can be.

Who 's the darling little girl
    Everybody loves to hear ?
She it is whose pleasant voice
    Falls like music on the ear.

Who 's the darling little girl
    Everybody loves to know ?
She it is whose arts and thoughts
    All are pure as whitest snow.

Who 's the darling little girl
    Even Jesus Christ can love ?
She it is who, meek and good,
    Daily grows like Him above.
              MELODIES FOR CHILDHOOD.

IS IT YOU?

THERE is a child, — a boy or girl, —
    I 'm sorry it is true, —
Who does n't mind when spoken to :
    Is it ? — it is n't you !
    O no, it can't be you !

3

I know a child, — a boy or girl, —
  I 'm loth to say I do, —
Who struck a little playmate child :
  Was it ? — it was n't you !
  I hope that was n't you !

I know a child, — a boy or girl, —
  I hope that such are few, —
Who told a lie ; yes, told a lie !
  Was it ? — it was n't you !
  It cannot be 't was you !

There is a boy, — I know a boy, —
  I cannot love him though, —
Who robs the little birdies' nests ;
  Is it ? — it can't be you !
  That bad boy can't be you !

A girl there is, — a girl I know, —
  And I could love her too,
But that she is so proud and vain ;
  Is it ? — it can't be you !
  That surely is n't you !

Mrs. Goodwin.

THE ROBIN-REDBREASTS.

Two Robin-redbreasts built their nests
  Within a hollow tree ;

The hen sat quietly at home,
　　The cock sang merrily ;
And all the little young ones said :
　　" Wee, wee, wee, wee, wee, wee."

One day (the sun was warm and bright,
　　And shining in the sky)
Cock-robin said : " My little dears,
　　'T is time you learned to fly ; "
And all the little young ones said :
　　" I 'll try, I 'll try, I 'll try."

I know a child, — and who she is
　　I 'll tell you by and by, —
When mamma says : " Do this," or " that,"
　　She says : " What for ? " and " Why ? "
She 'd be a better child by far
　　If she would say : " I 'll try."

AUNT EFFIE'S RHYMES.

GOOD MORNING.

" O, I am so happy ! " a little girl said,
As she sprang, like a lark, from her low trundle-bed ;
" 'T is morning, bright morning : good morning, papa.
O give me one kiss for good morning, mamma :
Only just look at my pretty canary,
Chirping his sweet good morning to Mary.

The sun is peeping straight into my eyes, —
Good morning to you, Mister Sun, for you rise
Early to wake up my birdie and me,
And make us as happy as happy can be."

" Happy you may be, my dear little girl ; "
And the mother stroked softly each clustering curl :
" Happy you can be ; but think of the One
Who wakened, this morning, both you and the sun."
The little girl turned her bright eyes with a nod :
" Mamma, may I say ' Good morning ' to God ? "
" Yes, little darling one, surely you may ;
Kneel, as you kneel every morning to pray."
Mary knelt solemnly down, with her eyes
Looking up earnestly into the skies ;

And two little hands, that were folded together,
Softly she laid on the lap of her mother :
" Good morning, dear Father in heaven," she said ;
" I thank Thee for watching my snug little bed ;
For taking good care of me all the dark night,
And waking me up with the beautiful light.
O keep me from naughtiness all the long day,
Dear Saviour, who taught little children to pray ! "

An angel looked down in the sunshine and smiled,
But she saw not the angel, — that beautiful child !

I WILL BE GOOD TO-DAY.

" I WILL be good, dear mother,"
  I heard a sweet child say ;
" I will be good ; now watch me, —
  I will be good all day."

She lifted up her bright young eyes,
  With a soft and pleasing smile ;
Then a mother's kiss was on her lips,
  So pure and free from guile.

And when night came, that little one
  In kneeling down to pray,
Said, in a soft and whispering tone :
  " Have I been good to-day ? "

O, many, many bitter tears,
  'T would save us, did we say,
Like that dear child, with earnest heart :
  " I will be good to-day."

GOD MADE ME.

I now am but a little child ;
  My hands are weak, my strength is small ;
Yet I can seek, and I can love,
  The Lord Almighty, God of all.

He gave my life to me at first ;
　He loves the little child He made ;
He keeps me safe through all the day,
　And guards me when in sleep I 'm laid.

If I obey and love His law,
　He 'll teach me all I need to know ;
And take me in His arms on high
　When I have lived my life below.
HYMNS FOR YOUNG CHILDREN.

LITTLE DANDELION.

GAY little Dandelion
　Lights up the meads,
Swings on her slender foot,
　Telleth her beads.
Lists to the robin's note
　Poured from above ;
Wise little Dandelion
　Asks not for love.

Cold lie the daisy banks,
　Clad but in green,
Where, in the days agone,
　Bright hues were seen.
Wild pinks are slumbering,
　Violets delay ;

True little Dandelion
  Greeteth the May.

Brave little Dandelion !
  Fast falls the snow,
Bending the daffodil's
  Haughty head low.
Under that fleecy tent,
  Careless of cold,
Blithe little Dandelion
  Counteth her gold.

Meek little Dandelion
  Groweth more fair,
Till dries the amber dew
  Out from her hair.
High rides the thirsty sun,
  Fiercely and high ;
Faint little Dandelion
  Closeth her eye !

Pale little Dandelion,
  In her white shroud,
Heareth the angel breeze
  Call from the cloud !
Tiny plumes fluttering,
  Make no delay !
Little winged Dandelion
  Soareth away !

LILY OF THE VALLEY.

COME, my love, and do not spurn
From a little flower to learn;
See the lily on its bed,
Hanging down its modest head,
While it scarcely can be seen,
Folded in its leaf of green.

Yet we love the lily well,
For its sweet and pleasant smell;
And would rather call it ours,
Than many other gayer flowers;
Pretty lilies seem to be
Emblems of humility.

Come, my love, and do not spurn
From a little flower to learn;
Let your temper be as sweet,
As the lily at your feet;
Be as gentle, be as mild,
Be a modest, humble child.

'T is not beauty that we prize, —
Like a summer's flower it dies;
But humility will last,
Fair and sweet when beauty 's past.;
And the Saviour from above,
Views a humble child with love.

THE JOURNEY.

DEAR mother, how pretty the moon looks to-night,
   She was never so cunning before!
Her two little horns are so sharp and so bright,
   I hope she won't grow any more!

If I were up there, with you and my friends,
   We'd have a nice rock, do you see;
We'd sit in the middle, and hold at both ends,
   O, what a bright cradle 't would be!

We'd call to the stars to get out of our way,
   Lest we should rock over their toes;
And then we would stay till the dawn of day,
   And see where the pretty moon goes.

And then we would float through the beautiful skies,
   And then through bright clouds we would roam,
And see the sun set, and see the sun rise,
   And on the next rainbow come home.

CHOICE POEMS.

LADY MOON.

'I see the Moon, and the Moon sees me,
  God bless the Moon, and God bless me."— *Old Rhyme.*

LADY Moon, Lady Moon, where are you roving?
   Over the sea.
Lady Moon, Lady Moon, whom are you loving?
   All that love me.

Are you not tired with rolling, and never
    Resting to sleep?
Why look so pale, and so sad, as forever
    Wishing to weep?

Ask me not this, little child, if you love me;
    You are too bold;
I must obey my dear Father above me,
    And do as I'm told.

Lady Moon, Lady Moon, where are you roving?
    Over the sea.
Lady Moon, Lady Moon, whom are you loving?
    All that love me.

R. M. MILNES.

LADY BIRD.

LADY bird! lady bird! fly away home,
    The field-mouse has gone to her nest,
The daisies have shut up their sweet, sleepy eyes,
    And the bees and the birds are at rest.

Lady bird! lady bird! fly away home,
    The glow-worm is lighting her lamp,
The dew's falling fast, and your fine speckled wings
    Will be wet with the close-clinging damp.

Lady bird! lady bird! fly away home,
 The fairy bells tinkle afar,
Make haste, or they 'll catch you, and harness you fast,
 With a cobweb, to Oberon's car.

CHOICE POEMS.

THE WATCH-DOG.

FROM "WILLIE WINKIE."

Bow-wow-wow!
It 's the great watch-dog,
I ken by his honest bark;
Bow-wow-wow!
Says the great watch-dog
When he hears a foot in the dark.

Not a breath can stir
But he 's up with a whirr!
And a big bow-wow gives he;
And, with tail on end,
He 'll the house defend
Far better than lock or key.

When we sleep sound,
He takes his round,
A sentry o'er us all.
Through the long, dark night,
Till broad daylight,
He scares the thieves from our wall.

But through the whole day
With the bairns he 'll play,
And gambol in the sun;
On his back astride
They may safely ride,
For well he loves their fun.

By all he 's kenned
As a faithful friend,
No flattering tongue has he;
And we may all learn
From the great watch-dog
Both faithful and fond to be.

ALEXANDER SMART.

LITTLE CHILDREN, LOVE ONE ANOTHER.

A LITTLE girl, with a happy look,
Sat slowly reading a ponderous book,
All bound with velvet, and edged with gold,
And its weight was more than a child could hold;
Yet dearly she loved to ponder it o'er,
And every day she prized it more;
For it said,—and she looked at her smiling mother,—
It said: "Little children, love one another."

She thought it was beautiful in the book,
And the lesson home to her heart she took.
She walked on her way with a trusting grace,
And a dovelike look in her meek young face,

Which said, just as plain as words could say :
The Holy Bible I must obey ;
So, mamma, I 'll be kind to my darling brother,
For " little children must love each other."

I am sorry he 's naughty and will not play,
But I 'll love him still ; for I think the way
To make him gentle and kind to me
Will be better shown, if I let him see
I strive to do what I think is right.
And thus, when we kneel in prayer to-night,
I will clasp my arms about my brother,
And say : " Little children, love one another."

The little girl did as her Bible taught,
And pleasant, indeed, was the change it wrought ;
For the boy looked up in glad surprise,
To meet the light of her loving eyes :
His heart was full ; he could not speak,
But he pressed a kiss on his sister's cheek ;
And God looks down on the happy mother
Whose " little children loved one another."

BEING KIND AND AFFECTIONATE.

THE God of heaven is pleased to see
A little family agree ;
And will not slight the praise they bring,
When loving children join to sing.

For love and kindness please him more
Than if we give him all our store ;
And children here, who dwell in love,
Are like his happy ones above.

The gentle child, who tries to please,
Dislikes to quarrel, fret, and tease,
And would not say an angry word, —
That child is pleasing to the Lord.

Great God ! forgive whenever we
Forget thy will and disagree ;
And grant that each of us may find
The sweet delight of being kind.

NOT READY FOR SCHOOL.

Pray, where is my hat, — it is taken away,
   And my shoe-strings are all in a knot ;
I can't find a thing where it should be to-day,
   Though I 've hunted in every spot.

Do, Rachel, just look for my Atlas up stairs,
   My Æsop is somewhere there too ;
And sister, just brush down these troublesome hairs,
   And mother just fasten my shoe.

And sister, beg father to write an excuse,
  But stop, he will only say "No";
And go on with a smile, and keep reading the news,
  While everything bothers me so.

My satchel is heavy, and ready to fall,
  This old pop-gun is breaking my map;
I'll have nothing to do with the pop-gun or ball,
  There's no playing for such a poor chap.

The town-clock will strike in a minute, I fear,
  Then away to the foot I must sink;
There — look at my Carpenter tumbled down here,
  And my Worcester covered with ink.

I wish I'd not lingered at breakfast the last,
  Though the toast and the butter were fine;
I think that our Edward must eat pretty fast,
  To be off when I have n't done mine.

Now Edward and Henry protest they won't wait,
  And beat on the door with their sticks;
I suppose they will say *I was dressing too late;*
  To-morrow, *I'll be up at six.*

MRS. GILMAN.

BUSY LITTLE HUSBANDMAN.

I 'M a little husbandman,
Work and labor hard I can ;
I 'm as happy all the day
At my work as if 't were play :
Though I 've nothing fine to wear,
Yet for that I do not care.

When to work I go along,
Singing loud my morning song,
With my wallet on my back,
And my wagon-whip to crack,
O, I 'm thrice as happy then
As the idle gentleman.

I 've a hearty appetite,
And I soundly sleep at night ;.
Down I lie content, and say
I 've been useful all the day :
I 'd rather be a ploughboy than
A useless little gentleman.

KINDNESS TO SERVANTS.

NURSERY SONGS OF SCOTLAND.

Now what was that you said to May
So pettishly yestreen ?
O, well you may feel shame to tell
How saucy you have been.
There 's nothing spoils a bonny face
Like sulks, in old or young,
And what can fit a lassie worse,
Than an ill-bred, saucy tongue ?

It 's not your part to scold at May,
To you she 's aye been kind,
And oft she 's sung you to your sleep,
Long, long ere you can mind.
She cooks the meat, she does the work,
She cleans when you but soil,
And what would helpless bairnies be,
Without the hands that toil ?

The kindly look, the gentle word,
Make friends of all who live,
And give a charm to every face
That nothing else can give.
It 's well for bairns to have a friend,
Who watches them with care, —
For when in fault, — they learn from him
In future to beware.

ALEXANDER SMART.

3

D

THE LITTLE TREE

THAT WANTED TO HAVE OTHER LEAVES.

A LITTLE tree stood up in the wood,
  In bright and dirty weather;
And nothing but needles it had for leaves,
  From top to bottom together.
The needles stuck about,
And the little tree spoke out: —

"My companions all have leaves
  Beautiful to see,
While I 've nothing but these needles;
  No one touches me.
Might I have my fortune told,
All my leaves should be pure gold."

The little tree 's asleep by dark,
  Awake by earliest light;
And now its golden leaves you mark;
  There was a sight!
The little tree says: " Now I 'm set high;
No tree in the wood has gold leaves but I."

And now again the night came back;
  Through the forest there walked a Jew;
With great thick beard and great thick sack,
  And soon the gold leaves did view.

He pockets them all, and away does fare,
Leaving the little tree quite bare.

The little tree speaks up distressed:
  "Those golden leaves how I lament!
I'm quite ashamed before the rest,
  Such lovely dress to them is lent.
Might I bring one more wish to pass,
I would have my leaves of the clearest glass."

The little tree sleeps again at dark,
  And wakes with the early light;
And now its glass leaves you may mark;—
  There was a sight!
The little tree says: "Now I'm right glad,
No tree in the wood is so brightly clad."

There came up now a mighty blast,
  And a furious gale it blew;
It swept among the trees full fast,
  And on the glass leaves it flew.
There lay the leaves of glass
All shivered on the grass.

The little tree complains:
  "My glass lies on the ground;
Each other tree remains
  With its green dress all round.
Might I but have my wish once more,
I would have of those good green leaves good store."

Again asleep is the little tree,
  And early wakes to the light;
He is covered with green leaves fair to see, —
  He laughs outright;
And says : "I am now all nicely drest,
Nor need be ashamed before the rest."

And now, with udders full,
  Forth a wild she-goat sprung,
Seeking for herbs to pull,
  To feed her young.
She sees the leaves, nor makes much talk,
But strips all clear to the very stalk.

The little tree again is bare,
  And thus to himself he said :
" No longer for my leaves I care,
  Whether green, or yellow, or red.
If I had but my needles again,
I would never more scold or complain."

The little tree slept sad that night,
  And sadly opened his eye ; —
He sees himself in the sun's first light,
  And laughs as if he would die.
And all the trees in a roar burst out;
But the little tree little cared for their flout.

What made the little tree laugh like mad ?
  And what set the rest in a roar ?

In a single night soon back he had
    Every needle he had before.
And everybody may see them such;
Go out and look, — but do not touch.

        Why not, I pray ?
        They prick, some say.
            RÜCKERT, TRANS. BY DR. FROTHINGHAM.

THE APPLE-TREE.

OLD John had an apple-tree, healthy and green,
Which bore the best baldwins that ever were seen,
    So juicy, and mellow, and red ;
And when they were ripe, as old Johnny was poor,
He sold them to children that passed by his door
    To buy him a morsel of bread.

Little Dick, his next neighbor, one often might see,
With longing eye viewing this nice apple-tree,
    And wishing an apple would fall ;
One day, as he stood in the heat of the sun,
He began thinking whether he might not take one,
    And then he looked over the wall.

And as he again cast his eye on the tree,
He said to himself, " O, how nice they would be,
    So cool and refreshing to-day !
The tree is so full, and I'd only take one,

And old John won't see, for he is not at home,
   And nobody is in the way."

But stop, little boy, take your hand from the bough,
Remember, though old John can't see you just now,
   And no one to chide you is nigh,
There is ONE, who by night, just as well as by day,
Can see all you do, and can hear all you say,
   From his glorious throne in the sky.

O then, little boy, come away from the tree,
Content, hot or weary, or thirsty to be,
   Or anything rather than steal!
For the great God, who even through darkness can look,
Writes down every crime we commit, in his book,
   However we think to conceal.

                      JANE TAYLOR.

WHO STOLE THE BIRD'S-NEST?

   TE-WHIT! te-whit! te-whee!
   Will you listen to me?
   Who stole four eggs I laid,
   And the nice nest I made?

   Not I, said the cow, moo-oo!
   Such a thing I'd never do.
   I gave for you a wisp of hay,

And did not take your nest away.
Not I, said the cow, moo-oo!
Such a thing I 'd never do.

Te-whit! te-whit! te-whee!
Will you listen to me?
Who stole four eggs, I laid,
And the nice nest I made?

Bob-a-link! bob-a-link!
Now what do you think?
Who stole a nest away
From the plum-tree to-day?

Not I, said the dog, Bow-wow!
I would n't be so mean as that, now;
I gave hairs the nest to make,
But the nest I did not take.
Not I, said the dog, Bow-wow!
I would n't be so mean as that, now!

Te-whit! te-whit! te-whee!
Will you listen to me?
Who stole four eggs I laid,
And the nice nest I made?

Bob-a-link! Bob-a-link!
Now what do you think?
Who stole a nest away,
From the plum-tree to-day?

Coo-coo! coo-coo! coo-coo!
Let me speak a word, too;
Who stole that pretty nest
From little yellow-breast?

Not I, said the sheep, O no,
I would n't treat a poor bird so;
I gave the wool the nest to line,
But the nest was none of mine.
Baa! baa! said the sheep; O no,
I would n't treat a poor bird so.

Te-whit! te-whit! te-whee!
Will you listen to me?
Who stole four eggs I laid,
And the nice nest I made?

Bob-a-link! Bob-a-link!
Now what do you think?
Who stole a nest away,
From the plum-tree to-day?

Coo-coo! coo-coo! coo-coo!
Let me speak a word, too,
Who stole that pretty nest
From little yellow-breast?

Caw! caw! cried the crow,
I should like to know
What thief took away
A bird's nest to-day?

Cluck! cluck! cluck! said the hen,
Don't ask me again,
Why, I have n't a chick
Would do such a trick;
We all gave her a feather,
And she wove them together;
I'd scorn to intrude
On her and her brood.
Cluck! cluck! said the hen,
Don't ask me again.

Chirr-a-whirr! chirr-a-whirr!
We'll make a great stir!
Let us find out his name,
And all cry for shame!

I would not rob a bird,
 Said little Mary Green;
I think I never heard
 Of anything so mean.
'T is very cruel, too,
 Said little Alice Neal;
I wonder if he knew
 How sad the bird would feel?

A little boy hung down his head,
And went and hid behind the bed,
For he stole that pretty nest
From poor little yellow-breast;
And he felt so full of shame,
He did n't like to tell his name.

CHOICE POEMS.

THE BEETLE.

Who 'll catch the Beetle ?
" I," says Peter Spring,
" I 'll seize it by the wing,
I 'll catch the Beetle ! "

Who 'll get a piece of thread ?
" I," says Dicky Bluff,
" I 'll do it quick enough,
I 'll tie it round his leg."

Who 'll run and hold the string ?
" We 'll *all* take turns to run,
And have some royal fun,
We 'll *all* hold the string."

Who loves to hear him buzz ?
" We do," says Lu and Dick,
" *We* like this funny trick,
We love to hear him buzz ! "

But who is coming along ?
A Giant large and strong,
Ah, Peter, Dick, and Lu,
He 's looking right at you !

Now towards you all he springs ;
And ties your legs with strings ;

He ties them one by one,
And tells you all to run.

He cries, " Run, run, Dick, Lucy, and Peter,
" And, remember, just so you served the Fig-eater ! "

MRS. GILMAN.

GIVE AS YOU'D TAKE.

NURSERY SONGS OF SCOTLAND.

MY bairnies dear, when you go out
With other bairns to play,
Take heed of everything you do,
Of every word you say ;
From tricky, wee, mischievous loons
Keep back, my bairns, keep back ;
And aye to all such usage give
As you would like to take.

To twist the mouth and call ill names
Is surely very bad ;
Then all such doings still avoid,
They 'd make your mother sad.
To shield the weakly from the strong,
Be neither slow nor slack,
And aye to all such usage give,
As you would like to take.

A kindly word, a soothing look,
Have ready aye for all ;
We are one Maker's handiwork,
He made us — great and small —
We 're all the children of his care ;
O, then for his dear sake
Be sure such usage still to give
As you would like to take.

ALEXANDER RODGER.

THE BIRD'S FUNERAL.

HERE, in these rosy bowers,
    Sleep, little bird ! we crave
A spot beneath the flowers
    To dig thy early grave.

So charming was thy singing !
    Thou wast to us so dear,
Thy voice has ceased its ringing,
    And we are weeping here.

Sweet May waked all her roses
    Thy thrilling notes to hear ;
And now with mourning posies
    We strew thy silent bier.

SONGS FROM THE GERMAN.

MY FATHER.

Who took me from my mother's arms,
And, smiling at her soft alarms,
Showed me the world, and nature's charms?
          My father.

Who made me feel and understand
The wonders of the sea and land,
And mark through all the Maker's hand?
          My father.

Who climbed with me the mountain height,
And watched my look of dread delight,
While rose the glorious orb of light?
          My father.

Who, from each flower and verdant stalk,
Gathered a subject for our talk,
To fill the long, delightful walk?
          My father.

Not on a poor worm would he tread,
Nor strike the little insect dead;
Who taught at once my heart and head?
          My father.

Who taught my early mind to know
The God from whom all blessings flow,
Creator of all things below?
          My father.

Soon, and before the mercy-seat,
Spirits made perfect, — we shall meet!
Then with what transports shall I greet
> My father.

> ANN TAYLOR.

MY MOTHER.

WHO fed me from her gentle breast,
And hushed me in her arms to rest,
And on my cheek sweet kisses pressed?
> My mother.

When sleep forsook my open eye,
Who was it sang sweet lullaby,
And rocked me that I should not cry?
> My mother.

Who sat and watched my infant head,
When sleeping on my cradle bed,
And tears of sweet affection shed?
> My mother.

When pain and sickness made me cry,
Who gazed upon my heavy eye,
And wept for fear that I should die?
> My mother.

Who dressed my doll in clothes so gay,
And taught me pretty how to play,
And minded all I had to say ?   .

> My mother.

Who ran to help me when I fell,
And would some pretty story tell,
Or kiss the place to make it well ?

> My mother.

Who taught my infant lips to pray,
And love God's holy book and day,
And walk in wisdom's pleasant way ?

> My mother.

And can I ever cease to be
Affectionate and kind to thee,
Who was so very kind to me ?

> My mother.

Ah ! no, the thought I cannot bear,
And if God please my life to spare,
I hope I shall reward thy care,

> My mother.

When thou art feeble, old, and gray,
My healthy arms shall be thy stay,
And I will soothe thy pains away,

> My mother.

And when I see thee hang thy head,
'T will be my turn to watch thy bed,
And tears of sweet affection shed,
           My mother.

For God, who lives above the skies,
Would look with sorrow in his eyes,
If I should ever dare despise
           My mother.
           ANN TAYLOR.

THE DOCTOR.

FROM WILLIE WINKIE.

O, DO not fear the doctor;
He comes to make you well,
To nurse you like a tender flower,
And pleasant tales to tell;
He brings the bloom back to your cheek,
The blithe blink to your eye,
An 't were not for the doctor,
My bonnie bairn might die.

O, who would fear the doctor,
His powder or his pill —
You just a wee bit swallow take,
And there 's an end of ill.
He 'll make you sleep sound as a top,

And rise up like a fly, —
An 't were not for the doctor,
My bonnie bairn might die.

A kind man is the doctor,
As many poor folk ken ;
He spares no toil by day or night
To ease them of their pain ;
And O, he loves the bairnies well
And grieves whene'er they cry, —
An 't were not for the doctor,
My bonnie bairn might die.

ALEXANDER SMART.

THE HAND-POST.

THE night was dark, the sun was hid
   Beneath the mountain gray:
And not a single star appeared,
   To shoot a silver ray.

Across the path the owlet flew,
   And screamed along the blast,
And onward with a quickened step,
   Benighted Henry passed.

At intervals, amid the gloom
   A flash of lightning played,
And showed the ruts with water filled,
   And the black hedge's shade.

E

Again in thickest darkness plunged,
  He groped his way to find ;
And now he thought he spied beyond
  A form of horrid kind.

In deadly white it upward rose,
  Of cloak or mantle bare,
And held its naked arms across,
  To catch him by the hair.

Poor Henry felt his blood run cold
  At what before him stood ;
But well, thought he, no harm, I 'm sure,
  Can happen to the good.

So calling all his courage up,
  He to the goblin went ;
And eager through the dismal gloom
  His piercing eyes he bent.

And when he came well nigh the ghost
  That gave him such affright,
He clapped his hands upon his side,
  And loudly laughed outright.

For 't was a friendly hand-post stood
  His wand'ring steps to guide ;
And thus he found that to the good
  No evil can betide.

And well, thought he, one thing I 've learnt,
　　Nor soon shall I forget,
Whatever frightens me again,
　　To march straight up to it.

And when I hear an idle tale
　　Of goblins and a ghost,
I 'll tell of this my lonely ride,
　　And the tall, white Hand-post.

ANN TAYLOR.

PART III.

NATURE.

THE BOOK OF NATURE.

THERE is a book, who runs may read,
　　Which heavenly truth imparts,
And all the lore its scholars need,
　　· Pure eyes and Christian hearts.

The works of God above, below,
    Within us, and around,
Are pages in that book to show
    How God himself is found.

The glorious sky, embracing all,
    Is like the Maker's love,
Wherewith encompassed, great and small
    In peace and order move.

The dew of heaven is like His grace,
    It steals in silence down ;
But where it lights, the favored place
    By richest fruits is known.

Thou, who hast given me eyes to see
    And love this sight so fair,
Give me a heart to find out Thee,
    And read Thee everywhere.

KEBLE.

———

THE BEGGAR.

A BEGGAR through the world am I, —
From place to place I wander by.
Fill up my pilgrim's scrip for me,
For Christ's sweet sake and charity !

A little of thy steadfastness,
Rounded with leafy gracefulness,
Old oak, give me, —
That the world's blasts may round me blow,
And I yield gently to and fro,
While my stout-hearted trunk below
And firm-set roots unshaken be.

Some of thy stern, unyielding might,
Enduring still through day and night
Rude tempest-shock and withering blight, —
That I may keep at bay
The changeful April sky of chance
And the strong tide of circumstance, —
Give me, old granite gray.

Some of thy pensiveness serene,
Some of thy never-dying green,
Put in this scrip of mine, —
That griefs may fall like snow-flakes light,
And deck me in a robe of white,
Ready to be an angel bright, —
O sweetly-mournful pine.

A little of thy merriment,
Of thy sparkling, light content,
Give me, my cheerful brook,
That I may still be full of glee
And gladsomeness, where'er I be,
Though fickle fate hath prisoned me
In some neglected nook.

4

Ye have been very kind and good
To me, since I 've been in the wood ;
Ye have gone nigh to fill my heart ;
But good by, kind friends, every one,
I 've far to go ere set of sun ;
Of all good things I would have part,
The day was high ere I could start,
And so my journey 's scarce begun.

Heaven help me! how could I forget
To beg of thee, dear violet!
Some of thy modesty,
That blossoms here as well, unseen,
As if before the world thou 'dst been,
O give, to strengthen me.

J. R. LOWELL.

GUESS WHAT I HAVE HEARD.

DEAR mother, guess what I have heard !
  O, it will soon be spring !
I 'm sure it was a little bird, —
  Mother I heard him sing.

Look at this little piece of green
  That peeps out from the snow,
As if it wanted to be seen, —
  'T will soon be spring, I know.

And O, come here, come here and look !
　How fast it runs along ! —
Here is a cunning little brook ;
　O, hear its pretty song !

1 know 't is glad the winter 's gone
　That kept it all so still,
For now it merrily runs on,
　And goes just where it will.

I feel just like the brook, I know ;
　It says, it seems to me, —
" Good by, cold weather, ice, and snow ;
　Now girls and brooks are free."

I love to think of what you said,
　Mother, to me last night,
Of this great world that God has made,
　So beautiful and bright.

And now it is the happy Spring
　No naughty thing I 'll do ;
I would not be the only thing
　That is not happy, too.

MRS. FOLLEN.

———

" BE kind to all you chance to meet,
　In field, or lane, or crowded street ;
　Anger and pride are both unwise —
　Vinegar never catches flies."

WHAT THEY ARE DOING.

" LITTLE Sparrow, come and say
What you 're doing all the day ? "

" O, I fly over hedges and ditches to find
A fat little worm, or a fly to my mind ;
And I carry it back to my own pretty nest
And the dear little pets that I warm with my breast ;
For until I can teach them the way how to fly,
If I were not to feed them, my darlings would die :
How glad they all are when they see me come home !
And each of them chirps, ' Give me some ! Give me
    some ! ' "

    " Little Lamb, come here and say
    What you 're doing all the day ? "

    " Long enough before you wake,
    Breakfast I am glad to take,
    In the meadow eating up
    Daisy, cowslip, buttercup ;
    Then about the fields I play,
    Frisk and scamper all the day ;
    When I 'm thirsty I can drink
    Water at the river's brink ;
    When at night I go to sleep,
    By my mother I must keep ;
    I am safe enough from cold
    At her side within the fold."

" Little Bee, come here and say
What you 're doing all the day ? "

" O, every day, and all day long,
Among the flowers you hear my song :
I creep in every bud I see,
And all the honey is for me ;
I take it to the hive with care
And give it to my brothers there,
That when the winter time comes on,
And all the flowers are dead and gone,
And when the wind is cold and rough,
The busy bees may have enough."

" Little Fly, come here and say
What you 're doing all the day ? "

" O, I am a gay and merry fly,
I never do anything — no, — not I.
I go where I like, and I stay where I please,
In the heat of sun, or the shade of the trees ;
On the window-pane, or the cupboard shelf;
And I care for nothing except myself :
I cannot tell, it is very true,
When the winter comes what I mean to do ;
And I very much fear, when I 'm getting old,
I shall starve with hunger, or die of cold."

RHYMES FOR LITTLE ONES.

THE GLADNESS OF NATURE.

Is this a time to be cloudy and sad,
When our mother Nature laughs around ;
When even the deep blue heavens look glad,
And gladness breathes from the blossoming ground ?

There are notes of joy from the hang-bird and wren,
And the gossip of swallows through all the sky ;
The ground-squirrel gayly chirps by his den,
And the wilding bee hums merrily by.

The clouds are at play in the azure space,
And their shadows at play on the bright green vale ;
And here they stretch to the frolic chase,
And there they roll on the easy gale.

There 's a dance of leaves in that aspen bower ;
There 's a titter of wind in that beechen tree ;
There 's a smile on the fruit, and a smile on the flower,
And a laugh from the brook that runs to the sea.

And look at the broadfaced sun, how he smiles
On the dewy earth that smiles in his ray,
On the breaking waters and gay young isles ; —
Ay, look ! and he 'll smile thy gloom away.

BRYANT.

WHAT I WOULD BE.

I WOULD not be an eagle fierce,
  With nest upon a rock,
Stealing the harmless little lambs
  From the poor shepherd's flock.

I would not be a moping owl,
  Snoring in bed all day,
And pouncing on the mice at night,
  When they come out to play.

No — I would be a lark, and mount
  From the daisy-spangled sod,
With twinkling wings to Heaven's gate,
  Singing the praise of God.

SONGS FROM THE GERMAN.

THE SONG OF THE GRASS.

HERE I come, creeping, creeping everywhere :
  By the dusty road-side,
  On the sunny hill-side,
  Close by the noisy brook,
  In every shady nook,
I come creeping, creeping everywhere.

Here I come, creeping, creeping everywhere :
   All around the open door,
   Where sit the aged poor,
   There where the children play,
   In the bright and merry May,
I come creeping, creeping everywhere.

Here I come, creeping, creeping everywhere :
   In the noisy city street
   My pleasant face you 'll meet,
   Cheering the sick at heart,
   Toiling his busy part,
Silently creeping, creeping everywhere.

Here I come, creeping, creeping everywhere :
   You cannot see me coming,
   Nor hear my low sweet humming,
   For in the starry night,
   And the glad morning light,
I come quietly, creeping everywhere.

Here I come, creeping, creeping everywhere :
   More welcome than the flowers,
   In summer's pleasant hours.
   The gentle cow is glad,
   And the merry bird not sad
To see me creeping, creeping everywhere.

Here I come, creeping, creeping everywhere :
   When you 're numbered with the dead,
   In your still and narrow bed,

In the happy Spring I 'll come,
And deck your silent home,
Creeping, silently creeping everywhere.

Here I come, creeping, creeping everywhere :
My humble song of praise
Most gratefully I raise
To Him at whose command
I beautify the land,
Creeping, silently creeping everywhere.

JOHN S. DWIGHT.

BIRDS.

O, THE sunny summer time !
O, the leafy summer time !
Merry is the bird's life,
When the year is in its prime !
Birds are by the waterfalls
Dashing in the rainbow spray ;
Everywhere, everywhere,
Light and lovely there are they !
Birds are in the forest old,
Building in each hoary tree ;
Birds are on the green hills ;
Birds are by the sea !

4 *   F

On the moor and in the fen,
  'Mong the whortleberries green ;
In the yellow furze-bush,
  There the joyous bird is seen ;
In the heather, on the hill ;
  All among the mountain thyme ;
By the little brook-sides,
  Where the sparkling waters chime ;
In the crag ; and on the peak,
  Splintered, savage, wild, and bare,
There the bird with wild wing
  Wheeleth through the air.

Wheeleth through the breezy air,
  Singing, screaming in his flight,
Calling to his bird-mate,
  In a troubleless delight !
In the green and leafy wood,
  Where the branching ferns up-curl,
Soon as is the dawning,
  Wakes the mavis and the merle ;
Wakes the cuckoo on the bough ;
  Wakes the jay with ruddy breast ;
Wakes the mother ringdove
  Brooding on her nest !

O, the sunny summer-time !
  O, the leafy summer-time !
Merry is the bird's life
  When the year is in its prime !

Some are strong and some are weak ;
   Some love day and some love night ;
But whate'er a bird is,
   Whate'er loves — it has delight
In the joyous song it sings ;
   In the liquid air it cleaves ;
In the sunshine, in the shower,
   In the nest it weaves !

MARY HOWITT.

SUMMER WOODS.

COME ye into the summer woods ;
   There entereth no annoy ;
All greenly wave the chestnut leaves,
   And the earth is full of joy.

I cannot tell you half the sights
   Of beauty you may see,
The bursts of golden sunshine,
   And many a shady tree.

There, lightly swung, in bowery glades,
   The honeysuckles twine ;
There blooms the rose-red campion,
   And the dark-red columbine.

There grows the four-leaved plant " true-love,"
  In some dusk woodland spot ;
There grows the enchanter's night-shade,
  And the wood forget-me-not.

And many a merry bird is there,
  Unscared by lawless men ;
The blue-winged jay, the woodpecker,
  And the golden-crested wren.

Come down, and ye shall see them all,
  The timid and the bold ;
For their sweet life of pleasantness,
  It is not to be told.

And far within that summer-wood,
  Among the leaves so green,
There flows a little gurgling brook,
  The brightest e'er was seen.

There come the little gentle birds,
  Without a fear of ill ;
Down to the murmuring water's edge
  And freely drink their fill !

And dash about and splash about,
  The merry little things ;
And look askance with bright black eyes,
  And flirt their dripping wings.

I 've seen the freakish squirrels drop
   Down from their leafy tree,
The little squirrels with the old, —
   Great joy it was to me !

And down unto the running brook
   I 've seen them nimbly go ;
And the bright water seemed to speak
   A welcome kind and low.

The nodding plants they bow their heads,
   As if, in heartsome cheer,
They spake unto those little things,
   " 'T is merry living here ! "

O, how my heart ran o'er with joy !
   I saw that all was good,
And how we might glean up delight
   All round us, if we would !

And many a wood-mouse dwelleth there,
   Beneath the old wood-shade,
And all day long has work to do,
   Nor is of aught afraid.

The green shoots grow above their heads,
   And roots so fresh and fine
Beneath their feet, nor is there strife
   'Mong them for *mine* and *thine*.

There is enough for every one,
  And they lovingly agree ;
We might learn a lesson, all of us,
  Beneath the green-wood tree !

MARY HOWITT.

LITTLE BELL.

"He prayeth well who loveth well
Both man and bird and beast."

PIPED the Blackbird on the beechwood spray,
" Pretty maid, slow wandering this way,
   What 's your name ? " quoth he —
" What 's your name ? O, stop and straight unfold
Pretty maid, with showery curls of gold ! "
   " Little Bell," said she.

Little Bell sat down beneath the rocks,
Tossed aside her gleaming golden locks,
   " Bonny bird ! " quoth she,
" Sing me your best song before I go."
" Here 's the very finest song I know,
   Little Bell," said he.

And the blackbird piped — you never heard
Half so gay a song from any bird —
   Full of quips and wiles,

Now so round and rich, now soft and slow,
All for love of that sweet face below,
    Dimpled o'er with smiles.

And the while the bonny bird did pour
His full heart out, freely o'er and o'er,
    'Neath the morning skies,
In the little childish heart below,
All the sweetness seemed to grow and grow,
And shine forth in happy overflow
    From the blue, bright eyes.

Down the dell she tripped ; and through the glade
Peeped the squirrel from the hazel shade,
    And from out the tree
Swung and leaped and frolicked, void of fear,
While bold Blackbird piped, that all might hear,
    " Little Bell ! " piped he.

Little Bell sat down amid the fern :
" Squirrel, Squirrel, to your task return ;
    Bring me nuts ! " quoth she.
Up, away ! the frisky squirrel hies —
Golden woodlights glancing in his eyes —
    And adown the tree,
Great ripe nuts, kissed brown by July sun,
In the little lap drop, one by one —
Hark, how Blackbird pipes to see the fun !
    "*Happy* Bell ! " pipes he.

Little Bell looked up and down the glade:
"Squirrel, Squirrel, from the nut-tree shade,
Bonny Blackbird, if you 're not afraid,
    Come and share with me!"
Down came Squirrel, eager for his fare,
Down came bonny Blackbird, I declare,
Little Bell gave each his honest share.
        Ah, the merry three!

And the while those frolic playmates twain
Piped and frisked from bough to bough again,
    'Neath the morning skies,
In the little childish heart below,
All the sweetness seemed to grow and grow,
And shine out, in happy overflow,
    From the blue, bright eyes.

By her snow-white cot, at close of day,
Knelt sweet Bell with folded palms, to pray —
    Very calm and clear
Rose the praying voice to where, unseen
In blue heaven, an angel shape serene
    Paused awhile to hear.

"What good child is this," the angel said,
"That with happy heart, beside her bed,
    Prays so lovingly!"
Low and soft, O very low and soft,
Crooned the Blackbird in the orchard croft,
    "Bell, *dear* Bell!" crooned he.

" Whom God's creatures love," the angel fair
Murmured, " God doth bless with angel's care ;
 Child, thy bed shall be
Folded safe from harm — love, deep and kind,
Shall watch around, and leave good gifts behind,
 Little Bell, for thee."

T. Westwood.

KINDNESS TO ANIMALS.

Turn, turn the hasty foot aside,
 Nor crush that helpless worm ;
The frame thy wayward looks deride,
 Required a God to form.

The common Lord of all that move,
 From whom thy being flowed,
A portion of his boundless love
 On that poor worm bestowed.

The sun, the moon, the stars he made,
 To all his creatures free ;
And spreads o'er earth the grassy blade
 For worms as well as thee.

Let them enjoy their little day,
 Their lowly bliss receive ;
O do not lightly take away
 The life thou canst not give.

Gisborn.

THE OAK-TREE.

SING for the Oak-tree,
　　The monarch of the wood ;
Sing for the Oak-tree,
　　That groweth green and good ;
That groweth broad and branching
　　Within the forest shade ;
That groweth now, and yet shall grow
　　When we are lowly laid !

The Oak-tree was an acorn once,
　　And fell upon the earth ;
And sun and showers nourished it,
　　And gave the Oak-tree birth.
The little sprouting Oak-tree !　　-
　　Two leaves it had at first,
Till sun and showers had nourished it,
　　Then out the branches burst.

The little sapling Oak-tree !
　　Its root was like a thread,
Till the kindly earth had nourished it,
　　Then out it freely spread :
On this side and on that side
　　It grappled with the ground ;
And in the ancient, rifted rock
　　Its firmest footing found.

The winds came, and the rain fell ;
   The gusty tempest blew ;
All, all were friends to the Oak-tree,
   And stronger yet it grew.
The boy that saw the acorn fall,
   He feeble grew and gray ;
But the oak was still a thriving tree.
   And strengthened every day !

Four centuries grows the Oak-tree,
   Nor doth its verdure fail ;
Its heart is like the iron-wood,
   Its bark like plated mail.
Now cut us down the Oak-tree,
   The monarch of the wood ;
And of its timbers stout and strong
   We 'll build a vessel good !

The Oak-tree of the forest
   Both east and west shall fly ;
And the blessings of a thousand lands
   Upon our ship shall lie !
For she shall not be a man of war,
   Nor a pirate shall she be ;
But a noble, Christian merchant ship,
   To sail upon the sea.

MARY HOWITT.

SUNSHINE.

I LOVE the sunshine everywhere, —
   In wood, and field, and glen ;
I love it in the busy haunts
   Of town-imprisoned men.

I love it when it streameth in
   The humble cottage-door,
And casts a checkered casement shade
   Upon the red-brick floor.

I love it where the children lie
   Deep in the clovery grass,
To watch among the twining roots
   The gold-green beetles pass.

I love it on the breezy sea,
   To glance on sail and oar,
While the great waves, like molten glass,
   Come leaping to the shore.

I love it on the mountain-tops,
   Where lies the thawless snow,
And half a kingdom, bathed in light,
   Lies stretching out below.

And when it shines in forest glades,
   Hidden and green and cool,
Through mossy boughs and veined leaves,
   How is it beautiful!

How beautiful on little streams,
   Where sun and shade at play,
Make silvery meshes, while the brook
   Goes singing on its way.

How beautiful, where dragon-flies
   Are wondrous to behold,
With rainbow wings of gauzy pearl,
   And bodies blue and gold!

How beautiful on harvest slopes,
   To see the sunshine lie;
Or on the paler reaped fields,
   Where yellow shocks stand high!

O yes! I love the sunshine:
   Like kindness or like mirth
Upon a human countenance
   Is sunshine on the earth!

Upon the earth, upon the sea,
   And through the crystal air,
On piled-up cloud, the gracious sun
   Is glorious everywhere!

                           MARY HOWITT.

ROBERT OF LINCOLN.

MERRILY singing on brier and weed,
   Near to the nest of his little dame,
Over the mountain-side or mead,
   Robert of Lincoln is telling his name:
      Bob-o'-link, Bob-o'-link,
      Spink, spank, spink;
Snug and safe in that nest of ours,
Hidden among the summer-flowers;
      Chee, chee, chee.

Robert of Lincoln is gayly drest,
   Wearing a bright-black wedding-coat;
White are his shoulders, and white his crest;
   Hear him call in his merry note,
      Bob-o'-link, Bob-o'-link,
      Spink, spank, spink;
Look what a nice new coat is mine,
Sure there was never a bird so fine;
      Chee, chee, chee.

Robert of Lincoln's Quaker wife,
   Pretty and quiet, with plain brown wings,
Passing at home a patient life,
   Broods in the grass while her husband sings,
      Bob-o'-link, Bob-o'-link;
Brood, kind creature, you need not fear
Thieves and robbers while I am here;
      Chee, chee, chee.

Modest and shy as a nun is she ;
    One weak chirp is her only note ;
Braggart, and prince of braggarts is he,
    Pouring boasts from his little throat —
Never was I afraid of man,
Catch me cowardly knaves, if you can.

Six white eggs on a bed of hay,
    Freckled with purple, a pretty sight!
There as the mother sits all day,
    Robert is singing with all his might, —
Nice good wife, that never goes out,
Keeping house while I frolic about.

Soon as the little ones chip the shell,
    Six wide mouths are open for food ;
Robert of Lincoln bestirs him well,
    Gathering seeds for the hungry brood.
This new life is likely to be
Hard for a young fellow like me.

Robert of Lincoln at length is made
    Sober with work, and silent with care ;
Off is his holiday garment laid
    Half forgotten that merry air, —
Nobody knows but my mate and I
Where our nest and our nestlings lie.

Summer wanes, — the children are grown:
    Fun and frolic no more he knows,

Robert of Lincoln 's a humdrum crone ;
　　Off he flies, and we sing as he goes, —
When you can pipe in that merry old strain,
Robert of Lincoln come back again.

　　　　　　　　　　　　　　　W. C. BRYANT

THANKFULNESS.

WHEN thou hast truly thanked thy God
　　For every blessing sent,
But little time will then remain
　　For murmur or lament.

THE WIND.

WHAT way does the wind come ? what way does he go
He rides over the water, and over the snow ;
Through wood, and through vale, and o'er rocky heigh
Which the goat cannot climb, takes his sounding fligh
He tosses about in every bare tree,
As, if you look up, you plainly may see ;
But how he will come, and whither he goes,
There 's never a scholar in England knows.

He will suddenly stop in a cunning nook,
And rings a sharp 'larum ; — but, if you should look,
There 's nothing to see but a cushion of snow,

Round as a pillow, and whiter than milk,
And softer than if it were covered with silk.
Sometimes he 'll hide in the cave of a rock,
Then whistle as shrill as the buzzard cock ;
— Yet seek him, — and what shall you find in the place ?
Nothing but silence and empty space ;
Save in a corner, a heap of dry leaves,
That he 's left, for a bed, to beggars or thieves !

As soon as 't is daylight, to-morrow with me,
You shall go to the orchard, and then you will see
That he has been there, and made a great rout
And cracked the branches, and strewn them about ;
Heaven grant that he spare but that one upright twig
That looked up at the sky so proud and big
All last summer, as well you know,
Studded with apples, a beautiful show !

Hark ! over the roof he makes a pause,
And growls as if he would fix his claws
Right in the slates, and with a huge rattle
Drive them down, like men in a battle :
— But let him range round ; he does us no harm,
We build up the fire, we 're snug and warm ;
Untouched by his breath, see the candle shines bright,
And burns with a clear and steady light ;
Books have we to read, — but that half stifled knell,
Alas ! 't is the sound of the eight o'clock bell.
— Come, now we 'll to bed ! and when we are there
He may work his own will, and what shall we care ?

5   G

He may knock at the door, — we 'll not let him in ;
May drive at the windows, — we 'll laugh at his din ;
Let him seek his own home wherever it be ;
Here 's a *cosey* warm house for Edward and me.

MARY LAMB.

THE KITTEN AND THE FALLING LEAVES.

SEE the kitten on the wall,
Sporting with the leaves that fall,
Withered leaves, one — two — and three,
From the lofty elder-tree !
Through the calm and frosty air
Of this morning, bright and fair,
Eddying round and round, they sink
Softly, slowly ; one might think,
From the motions that are made,
Every little leaf conveyed
Sylph or fairy hither tending,
To this lower world descending ;
Each invisible and mute
In his wavering parachute.

But the kitten, how she starts,
Crouches, stretches, paws, and darts,
First at one, and then its fellow,
Just as light and just as yellow ;
There are many now — now one —
Now they stop, and there are none.

What intenseness of desire
In her upward eye of fire !
With a tiger-leap, half-way
Now she meets the coming prey,
Lets it go as fast, and then
Has it in her power again.
Were her antics played i' the eye
Of a thousand standers-by,
Clapping hands with shout and stare,
What would little Tabby care
For the plaudits of the crowd ?
Over happy to be proud,
Over wealthy in the treasure
Of her own exceeding pleasure !

WORDSWORTH.

THE CORAL BRANCH.

I THOUGHT my branch of coral
  A pretty shrub might be,
Until I learned a little worm
  Had made it in the sea.

Down, down so deep,
Where dark waters sleep,
  The coral insect lives ;
But rests not there,
With toil and care
  It upward, upward strives.

It builds its coral palaces
    Than lofty hills more high,
And then the structure to complete,
    The little worm must die ;

Thus teaching me,
When coral I see,
    That dying I should leave
Some good work here
My friends to cheer,
    When o'er my tomb they grieve.

JACK FROST.

A BRIGHT little rogue jumped out of his bed,
With his rose-flushed cheek, and his golden hair
Curling and floating all over his head,
As if slumber had only been frolicking there.
He sprung to the window, and clapped his hands,
And a smile came up in his deep-blue eyes,
For a vision of other, and lovelier lands,
In still, dim beauty, before him lies !
The fairy garden — the glittering mosque,
The graceful bower and gay kiosk,
The lake, that sparkles in light serene,
Might mark the picture a Persian scene :
That cataract foaming ! — A drop of light !
Those cloud-capt mountains in miniature !

Why, a fly, in a twinkling, could climb the height,
Where Eastern idolaters knelt of yore!
But close to the temple — how came it there ? —
Is something that looks like a great white bear!
And gliding away on the sunniest edge
Of the garden bright, is a Lapland sledge!
The graceful reindeer is white as snow, —
And the reins and his antlers are silver, I know!
And see! on the seat of the gossamar car,
A dear little Laplander shines like a star,
With a cunning white boa, on her tiny blue dress —
What! fur among roses! she 'll melt, I guess.
She is rather too brilliant for nature ; no matter, —
We believe 't is the license of painters to flatter.
Willy knew by the tracing, strange and fair,
That a queer little artist, called Frost, had been there ;
He thought, too, he spied him, outside of the pane —
That funny old man — when he looked again,
With his twinkling eyes, keen, cold, and bright,
His pallet of pearl and pencil of light,
His pinions of fleece, with moonbeams inlaid,
And his three-cornered cap, of a diamond made.
He looked hard at Willy, as much as to say,
" I would give the best gem in my casket, to play
With your wild, bright curls, and your lip of rose,
Or to bite off the end of your dear little nose ! "
" No ! no ! Mr. Frost, you may peep if you please,
Over the mountains, and through the trees !
You may float in the clouds, through the deep midnight,
And play with your jewels of rainbow light !

You may dance on the lake with your twinkling feet,
Till it hardens beneath them, a silver sheet!
You may wave your wings o'er the woodland bloom,
And sprinkle their sparkles amid the gloom,
Till the whole wide forest, from towering pine
To baby-bush, with your snow-plumes shine!
You may look on the rivulet, murmuring by,
Till you charm it to sleep with your clear, cold eye,
And bid it forget its flowing.
You may do what you will, and I will not fear —
No! no! Mr. Frost, you shall not come here.
Mother, how cold it is growing!
No! no! Mr. Frost, you may bite, if you please,
The poor little shivering birds on the trees;
You may dig with the point of your cap in the earth,
Till you come to the place where the flowers have birth,
And tell them they must n't come up, — if they do,
You 'll pinch them all, till they 're black and blue!
You may frighten the lilies and roses;
You may bite the bush, the vine, the tree,
But, Mr. Jack Frost, you shall not bite *me!*
Mother, how cold my nose is!
No! no! Mr. Frost, you may eat the grass;
You may try your teeth upon window-glass,
Since you must do some mischief or other;
You may swallow the brooks, — and the deep, full sea,
You thirsty old fellow! your drink may be,
But, dear Mr. Jack Frost! please don't eat me!
O, give me my breakfast mother!"
The milk was lifted, for Willy to sip;

But he felt, just then, on his soft, warm lip,
A tiny touch, from a hand of ice,
And he put it away from his mouth in a trice.
What do you think he found in his cup ?
The poor little iceman himself peeped up.
Willy lifted the bowl — one draught he drew ; —
" And pray, Mr. Jack Frost, where are you ?
You need n't go diving and glancing about,
As if little Willy would let you come out."
Ah, Willy ! he drained the sweet cup with delight,
And when he had finished, he stared in affright,
He thought he should find him all snugly curled up,
The poor little painter ! within the deep cup.
Full sharply he looked — but Jack was not there,
And Willy cried out, " He 's gone, I declare !
While I drank, he jumped from the bowl, I know —
Mother, dear mother, did *you* see him go ?
You 're a coward, Jack Frost; and next time I meet you,
If you dare touch my lips, I will surely eat you."

CHOICE POEMS.

IT SNOWS.

It snows ! it snows ! from out the sky
The feathered flakes, how fast they fly.
Like little birds, that don't know why
They 're on the chase, from place to place,
While neither can the other trace.
It snows ! it snows ! a merry play
Is o'er us, on this heavy day !

As dancers in an airy hall,
That has n't room to hold them all,
While some keep up, and others fall,
The atoms shift, then, thick and swift,
They drive along to form the drift,
That waving up, so dazzling white,
Is rising like a wall of light.

But now the wind comes whistling loud,
To snatch and waft it as a cloud,
Or giant phantom in a shroud ;
It spreads ! it curls ! it mounts and whirls !
At length, a mighty wing unfurls ;
And then, away ! but, where, none knows,
Or ever will. — It snows ! it snows !

To-morrow will the storm be done ;
Then, out will come the golden sun :
And we shall see, upon the run
Before his beams, in sparkling streams,
What now a curtain o'er him seems.
And thus, with life, it ever goes ;
'T is shade and shine ! — It snows ! it snows !

H. F. GOULD.

'T is little acts of good or ill,
    That make our vast account.
No *one*, though great, does *all* God's will.
Small drops the caves of ocean fill ;
    And sands compose the mount.

IBID.

LOVING AND LIKING.

THERE 's more in words than I can teach :
Yet listen, Child ! — I would not preach ;
But only give some plain directions
To guide your speech and your affections.
Say not you *love* a roasted Fowl,
But you may love a screaming Owl,
And if you can, the unwieldy Toad
That crawls from his secure abode
Within the mossy garden-wall
When evening dews begin to fall.
O, mark the beauty of his eye :
What wonders in that circle lie !
So clear, so bright, our fathers said
He wears a jewel in his head !
And when, upon some showery day,
Into a path or public way,
A Frog leaps out from bordering grass,
Startling the timid as they pass,
Do you observe him, and endeavor
To take the intruder into favor ;
Learning from him to find a reason
For a light heart in a dull season.
And you may love him in the pool,
That is for him a happy school,
In which he swims, as taught by nature,
A pattern for a human creature,
Glancing amid the water bright,

5 *

And sending upward sparkling light.
Nor blush if o'er your heart be stealing
A love for things that have no feeling ;
The spring's first Rose, by you espied,
May fill your breast with joyful pride ;
And you may love the Strawberry flower,
And love the Strawberry in its bower ;
But when the fruit, so often praised
For beauty to your lip is raised,
Say not you *love* the delicate treat,
But *like* it, enjoy it, and thankfully eat.
Long may you love your pensioner Mouse,
Though one of a tribe that torment the house :
Nor dislike for her cruel sport the Cat,
That deadly foe of both mouse and rat :
Remember she follows the law of her kind,
And Instinct is neither wayward nor blind.
Then think of her beautiful gliding form,
Her tread that would not crush a worm,
And her soothing song by the winter fire,
Soft as the dying throb of the lyre.

I would not circumscribe your love :
It may soar with the eagle and brood with the dove,
May pierce the earth with the patient mole,
Or track the hedgehog to his hole.
Loving and liking are the solace of life,
They foster all joy, and extinguish all strife.
You love your father and your mother,
Your grown-up and your baby brother ;

You love your sister, and your friends,
And countless blessings which God sends :
And while these right affections play,
You LIVE each moment of your day ;
They lead you on to full content,
And likings fresh and innocent,
That store the mind, the memory feed,
And prompt to many a gentle deed :
But LIKINGS come, and pass away ;
'T is LOVE that remains till our latest day :
Our heavenward guide is holy love,
And it will be our bliss with saints above !

MARY LAMB.

THE BAREFOOT BOY.

BLESSINGS on thee, little man,
Barefoot boy, with cheek of tan !
With thy turned-up pantaloons,
And thy merry whistled tunes ;
With thy red lip, redder still
Kissed by strawberries on the hill ;
With the sunshine on thy face,
Through thy torn brim's jaunty grace :
From my heart I give thee joy —
I was once a barefoot boy !
Prince thou art — the grown-up man
Only is republican.

Let the million-dollared ride !
Barefoot, trudging at his side,
Thou hast more than he can buy,
In the reach of ear and eye —
Outward sunshine, inward joy :
Blessings on thee, barefoot boy !

O for boyhood's painless play,
Sleep that wakes in laughing day,
Health that mocks the doctor's rules,
Knowledge never learned in schools,
Of the wild-bee's morning chase,
Of the wild-flower's time and place,
Flight of fowl, and habitude
Of the tenants of the wood ;
How the tortoise bears his shell,
How the woodchuck digs his cell,
And the ground-mole sinks his well ;
How the robin feeds her young,
How the oriole's nest is hung ;
Where the whitest lilies blow,
Where the freshest berries grow,
Where the ground-nut trails its vine,
Where the wood-grape's clusters shine ;
Of the black wasp's cunning way,
Mason of his walls of clay,
And the architectural plans
Of gray hornet artisans ! —
For, eschewing books and tasks,
Nature answers all he asks ;

Hand in hand with her he walks,
Face to face with her he talks,
Part and parcel of her joy —
Blessings on the barefoot boy!

Cheerily, then, my little man,
Live and laugh, as boyhood can!
Though the flinty slopes be hard,
Stubble-speared the new-mown sward,
Every morn shall lead thee through
Fresh baptisms of the dew;
Every evening from thy feet
Shall the cool wind kiss the heat:
All too soon these feet must hide
In the prison cells of pride,
Lose the freedom of the sod,
Like a colt's for work be shod.
Happy if their track be found
Never on forbidden ground;
Happy if they sink not in
Quick and treacherous sands of sin.
Ah! that thou couldst know thy joy,
Ere it passes, barefoot boy!

J. G. WHITTIER.

TIRED OF PLAY.

TIRED of play ! tired of play !
What hast thou done this livelong day ?
The bird is hushed, and so is the bee,
The sun is creeping up steeple and tree ;
The doves have flown to the sheltering eaves,
And the nests are dark with the drooping leaves ;
Twilight gathers, and day is done ; —
How hast thou spent it, precious one ?

Playing ? — But what hast thou done beside,
To tell thy mother at eventide ?
What promise of morn is left unbroken ?
What kind word to thy playmate spoken ?
Whom hast thou pitied, and whom forgiven ?
How with thy faults has duty striven ?
What hast thou learned by field and hill,
By green-wood path, and by singing rill ?

There will come an eve to a longer day,
That will find thee tired, — but not of play.
Well for thee then, if thy lip can tell
A tale like this of a day spent well.
If thine open hand hath relieved distress,
If thy pity hath sprung at wretchedness,
If thou hast forgiven the sore offence,
And humbled thy heart with penitence ;
If Nature's voices have spoken to thee

With their holy meanings, eloquently ;
If every creature hath won thy love,
From the creeping worm to the brooding dove,
And never a sad, low-spoken word
Hath plead with thy human heart unheard, —
Then, when the night steals on as now,
It will bring relief to thine aching brow,
And with joy and peace at the thought of rest,
Thou wilt sink to sleep on thy mother's breast.

N. P. WILLIS.

NOT TO MYSELF ALONE.

" NOT to myself alone,"
The little opening flower transported cries, —
" Not to myself alone I bud and bloom ;
With fragrant breath the breezes I perfume,
And gladden all things with my rainbow dyes.
The bee comes sipping, every eventide,
His dainty fill ;
The butterfly within my cup doth hide
From threatening ill."

" Not to myself alone,"
The circling star with honest pride doth boast, —
" Not to myself alone I rise and set ;
I write upon night's coronal of jet
His power and skill who formed our myriad host ;

A friendly beacon at heaven's open gate,
    I gem the sky,
That man might ne'er forget, in every fate,
    His home on high."

" Not to myself alone,"
The heavy-laden bee doth murmuring hum, —
  " Not to myself alone, from flower to flower,
  I rove the wood, the garden, and the bower,
And to the hive at evening weary come :
    For man, for man, the luscious food I pile,
        With busy care,
    Content if I repay my ceaseless toil
        With scanty share."

" Not to myself alone,"
The soaring bird with lusty pinion sings, —
  " Not to myself alone I raise my song ;
  I cheer the drooping with my warbling tongue,
And bear the mourner on my viewless wings ;
    I bid the hymnless churl my anthem learn,
        And God adore ;
    I call the worldling from his dross to turn,
        And sing and soar."

" Not to myself alone,"
The streamlet whispers on its pebbly way, —
  " Not to myself alone I sparkling glide ;
  I scatter health and life on every side,
And strew the fields with herb and floweret gay.

I sing unto the common, bleak and bare,
    My gladsome tune ;
I sweeten and refresh the languid air
    In droughty June."

   " Not to myself alone,"
O man ! forget not thou — earth's honored priest,
  Its tongue, its soul, its lip, its pulse, its heart —
In earth's great chorus to sustain thy part !
Chiefest of guests at love's ungrudging feast,
  Play not the niggard ; spurn thy native clod,
    And *self* disown ;
  Live to thy neighbor, live unto thy God ;
    Not to thyself alone !

H

PART IV.

RELIGIOUS INSTRUCTION.

I. THE HEAVENLY FATHER.

THE MOTHER'S PRAYER.

FAIN, O my child, I 'd have thee know,
    The God whom angels love:
And teach thee feeble strains below,
    Akin to theirs above.

O when thy lisping tongue shall read
   Of truths divinely sweet,
May'st thou, a little child indeed,
   Sit down at Jesus' feet.

I 'll move thine ear, I 'll point thine eye —
   But ah ! the inward part —
Great God, the Spirit ! hear the sigh
   That trembles through my heart !

Break, with thy vital beam benign,
   O'er all the mental wild !
Bright o'er the human chaos shine,
   And sanctify my child.

MRS. VOKE.

TEACHING LITTLE CHILDREN.

O SAY not, think not, heavenly notes
   To childish ears are vain, —
That the young mind at random floats,
   And cannot reach the strain.

Was not our Lord a little child,
   Taught by degrees to pray,
By father dear and mother mild
   Instructed day by day ?

And loved he not of heaven to talk
  With children in his sight,
To meet them in his daily walk,
  And to his arms invite?

And though some tones be weak and low,
  What are all prayers beneath,
But cries of babes, that cannot know
  Half the deep thought they breathe?

In his own words we Christ adore;
  But angels, as we speak,
Higher above our meaning soar
  Than we o'er children weak.

And yet his words mean more than they,
  And yet he owns their praise;
O, think not that he turns away
  From infants' simple lays!

KEBLE.

THE PURE IN HEART.

BLEST are the pure in heart,
  For they shall see our God,
The secret of the Lord is theirs,
  Their soul is His abode.

Still to the lowly soul
  He doth Himself impart,
And for His temple and His throne
  Selects the pure in heart.

KEBLE

THE CHILD AND THE ANGELS.

THE Sabbath's sun was setting low,
  Amidst the clouds at even ;
" Our Father," breathed a voice below, —
  Father, who art in heaven."

Beyond the earth, beyond the clouds,
  Those infant words were given ;
" Our Father," angels sang aloud. —
  " Father, who art in heaven."

" Thy kingdom come," still from the ground,
  That child-like voice did pray ;
" Thy kingdom come," God's hosts resound,
  Far up the starry way.

" Thy will be done," with little tongue,
  That lisping love implores ;
" Thy will be done," the angelic throng
  Sing from the heavenly shores.

" Forever," still those lips repeat,
   Their closing evening prayer ;
" Forever," floats in music sweet,
   High 'midst the angels there."

CHARLES SWAIN.

GOD OUR FATHER.

WE are not orphans on the earth,
   Though friends and parents die ;
One Parent never bows to death, —
   One Friend is ever nigh.

Even he who lit the stars of old,
   And filled the ocean broad,
Whose works and ways are manifold, —
   Our father is our God.

There comes no change upon his years,
   No failure to his hand ;
His love will lighten all our cares,
   His law our steps command.

May Christ who for our sakes the gloom
   Of death's dark valley trod,
Bring us all safe at last to him, —
   Our Father and our God!

SUNDAY-SCHOOL HYMNS.

GOD IS NEAR.

I WILL not fear,
For God is near,
Through the dark night,
As in the light ;
And while I sleep,
Safe watch will keep,
Why should I fear,
When God is near ?

HYMNS FOR LITTLE ONES AT HOME.

FEAR NOT.

YEA, fear not, fear not little ones ;
   There is in heaven an Eye
That looks with yearning fondness down
   On all the paths ye try.

'T is He who guides the sparrow's wing,
   And guards her little brood ;
Who hears the ravens when they cry,
   And fills them all with food.

'T is He who clothes the field with flowers,
   And pours the light abroad ;
'T is He who numbers all your hours,
   Your Father and your God.

Ye are the chosen of his love,
   His most peculiar care;
And will he guide the fluttering dove,
   And not regard your prayer?

Nay, fear not, fear not, little ones;
   There is in heaven an Eye
That looks with yearning fondness down
   On all the paths you try.

He 'll keep you when the storm is wild,
   And when the flood is near;
O trust him, trust him as a child,
   And you have naught to fear!

GOD SEES ME.

THROUGH all the busy daylight, through all the quiet
    night,
Whether the stars in the sky, or the sun is shining
    bright;
In the nursery, in the parlor; in the street, or on the
    stair, —
Though I may seem to be alone, yet God is always
    there.
        Whatever I may do,
          Wherever I may be,
        Although I see him not,
          Yet God sees me.

He knows each word I mean to speak, before the word
    is spoken ;
He knows the thoughts within my heart, although I give
    no token.
When I am naughty, then I grieve my Heavenly Father's
    love ;
And, every time I really try, he helps me from above.
        Whatever I may do,
          Wherever I may be,
        Although I see him not,
         Yet God sees me.

I have kind and tender parents ; I have many loving
    friends :
But none love me as God loves me ; and all that's good
    he sends.
I will walk as God shall lead me, while the sun is in the
    sky ;
And lay me down, and sleep in peace, beneath his
    watchful eye.
        Whatever I may do,
          Wherever I may be,
        Although I see him not,
        Yet God sees me.

HYMNS FOR YOUNG CHILDREN.

GOD LOVES ME.

God cares for every little child
   That on this large earth liveth:
He gives them homes and food and clothes;
   And more than these God giveth; —

He gives them all their loving friends;
   He gives each child its mother;
He gives them all the happiness
   Of loving one another;

He makes the earth all beautiful;
   He makes thine eyes to see;
And touch and hearing, taste and smell,
   He gives them all to thee.

What can a little child give God?
   From his bright heavens above
The great God smiles, and reaches down
   To take his children's love.

HYMNS FOR YOUNG CHILDREN.

GOD'S CARE.

WHAT secret hand, at morning light,
   Softly unseals mine eye,

Draws back the curtain of the night,
   And opens earth and sky ?

'T is thine, my God, — the same that kept
   My resting hours from harm ;
No ill came nigh me, for I slept
   Beneath the Almighty's arm.

'T is thine my daily bread that brings,
   Like manna scattered round,
And clothes me, as the lily springs
   In beauty from the ground.

In death's dark valley though I stray,
   'T would there my steps attend,
Guide with the staff my lonely way,
   And with the rod defend.

May that sure hand uphold me still
   Through life's uncertain race,
To bring me to thy holy hill,
   And to thy dwelling-place.

                       MONTGOMERY.

GOD IS GOOD.

God is good ! each perfumed flower,
   The smiling fields, the dark green wood,

The insect, fluttering for an hour, —
    All things proclaim that God is good.

I hear it in each breath of wind;
    Hills that have for ages stood,
And clouds, with gold and silver lined,
    Are still repeating, God is good.

Each little rill, that many a year
    Has the same verdant path pursued,
And every bird, in accents clear,
    Joins in the song, that God is good.

The restless sea, with haughty roar,
    Calms each wild wave and billow rude,
Retreats submissive from the shore,
    And swells the chorus, " God is good."

The countless hosts of twinkling stars
    Sing his praise with light renewed;
The rising sun each day declares,
    In rays of glory, God is good.

The moon that walks in brightness, says
    That God is good! — and man, endued
With power to speak his Maker's praise,
    Should still repeat that God is good.

                      MRS. FOLLEN.

WHO TAKES CARE.

IN winter where can be the flowers,
  The leaves that look so green ?
There 's not a bud in all the bowers,
  Nor daisy to be seen.

And who will bring them back again,
  When pleasant spring comes out ?
And plant them up and down the lane,
  And spread them all about ?

And who will bring the little lambs
  With wool as soft as silk,
And teach them how to know their dams,
  And where to find the milk ?

And who will teach the little birds
  To build their nests on high,
And, though they cannot speak in words,
  To teach their young to fly ?

The Lord in Heaven — 't is there he dwells
  Who all these things can do ;
And his own book, the Bible, tells
  Much more about Him too.

                    SACRED SONGS FOR SUNDAY SCHOOLS.

FL●WERS.

God might have made the earth bring forth
  Enough for great and small,
The oak-tree, and the cedar-tree,
  Without a flower at all.

He might have made enough, enough
  For every want of ours ;
For luxury, medicine, and toil,
  And yet have made no flowers.

The clouds might give abundant rain,
  The nightly dews might fall,
And the herb that keepeth life in man,
  Might yet have drunk them all.

Then wherefore, wherefore were they made,
  And dyed with rainbow light,
All fashioned with supremest grace,
  Upspringing day and night ?

Springing in valleys green and low,
  And on the mountains high ;
And in the silent wilderness,
  Where no man passes by ?

6 *   I

Our outward life requires them not,
  Then wherefore had they birth ?
To minister delight to man ;
  To beautify the earth ;

To comfort man, — to whisper hope
  Whene'er his faith is dim ;
For whoso careth for the flowers,
  Will care much more for him !

MARY HOWITT.

CHILDREN IN CHURCH.

WHEN to the house of God we go,
  To hear his word and sing his love,
We ought to worship him below,
  As saints and angels do above.

They stand before his presence now,
  And praise him better far than we, —
Who only at his footstool bow,
  And love him whom we cannot see.

But God is present everywhere,
  And watches all our thoughts and ways :
He marks who humbly join in prayer,
  And who sincerely sing his praise.

The triflers, too, his eye can see,
   Who only seem to take a part ;
They move the lip and bend the knee,
   But do not seek him with the heart.

O, may we never trifle so,
   Nor lose the days our God has given ;
But learn, by Sabbaths here below,
   To spend eternity in heaven.

Sunday-School Hymns.

SEEKING GOD.

We come in childhood's innocence,
   We come, as children, free !
We offer up, O God ! our hearts
   In trusting love to thee.

Well may we bend, in solemn joy,
   At thy bright courts above, —
Well may the grateful child rejoice
   In such a Father's love.

In joy we wake, in peace we sleep,
   Safe from all midnight harms,
Not folded in an angel's wings,
   But in a Father's arms.

We come not as the mighty come,
　Not as the proud we bow ;
But as the pure in heart should bend,
　Seek we thine altars now.

" Forbid them not," the Saviour said ; —
　In speechless rapture dumb,
We hear the call, — we seek thy face, —
　Father, we come ! — we come !

T. Gray, Jr.

THE BEST OFFERING.

Lord, what offering shall we bring,
　At thine altar when we bow ?
Hearts, the pure, unsullied spring
　Whence the kind affections flow ;

Soft compassion's feeling soul,
　By the melting eye expressed ;
Sympathy, at whose control
　Sorrow leaves the wounded breast.

Willing hands to lead the blind,
　Bind the wounded, feed the poor ;
Love, embracing all our kind,
　Charity, with liberal store.

Teach us, O thou heavenly King!
  Thus to show our grateful mind;
Thus the accepted offering bring, —
  Love to thee and all mankind.

JANE TAYLOR.

THE GOLDEN RULE.

THUS said Jesus: " Go, and do
As thou wouldst be done unto."
— Here thy perfect duty see,
All that God requires of thee.

Wouldst thou then rejoice to find
Others generous, just, and kind?
Think upon these words, and do
As thou wouldst be done unto.

Wouldst thou, when thy faults are known,
Wish that pardon should be shown?
Be forgiving then, and do
As thou wouldst be done unto.

Shouldst thou helpless be, and poor,
Wouldst thou not for aid implore?
Think of others then, and be
What thou wouldst they should to thee.

For compassion if thou call,
Be compassionate to all ;
If thou wouldst affection find,
Be affectionate and kind.

If thou wouldst obtain the love
Of thy gracious God above ;
Then to all his children be
What thou wouldst they should to thee.

W. ROSCOE.

THE THRONE.

WHAT throne may bear the eternal God,
    Who fills unbounded space ?
What palace boast his bright abode,
    What world his dwelling-place ?

Ye stars, that gem yon glorious vault,
    Above, beneath, around !
Who most your Maker's praise exalt,
    Through nature's unknown bound ;

Ye sons of light, your God's first-born !
    Who saw, from distant spheres,
The dawn of this earth's natal morn,
    And all its future years ;

Ask ye where dwells the eternal God ?
  What planets bear his feet ?
What clustered suns are his abode,
  His burning, dazzling seat ?

There IS a throne your God will grace, —
  The pure and lowly heart ;
There will he choose his dwelling-place,
  And never thence depart.

HYMN.

THE glorious God who reigns on high,
Who formed the earth and built the sky,
Stoops from his throne in heaven to hear
A little infant's prattling prayer.

Father of all ! my Father too !
O make me good, and just, and true, —
Make me delight to learn thy word,
And love to pray and praise thee, Lord !

O may thy gracious presence bless
And guard my childhood's helplessness !
Be with me, as I grow in years,
And guide me through this vale of tears.

MRS. GILMAN.

"OUR FATHER WHO ART IN HEAVEN."

GREAT God, and wilt thou condescend
To be my father and my friend?
I a poor child, and thou so high,
The Lord of earth, and air, and sky!

Art thou my Father? Canst thou bear
To hear my poor, imperfect prayer?
Or stoop to listen to the praise
That such a little one can raise?

Art thou my Father? Let me be
A meek, obedient child to thee;
And try in word, and deed, and thought
To serve and please thee as I ought.

Art thou my Father? I'll depend
Upon the care of such a friend;
And only wish to do, and be,
Whatever seemeth good to thee.

Art thou my Father? Then at last,
When all my days on earth are past,
Send down and take me, in thy love,
To be thy better child above.

JANE TAYLOR.

II. THE GOOD SHEPHERD.

SWEDISH MOTHER'S HYMN.

BY FREDERIKA BREMER.

THERE sitteth a dove, so white and fair.
    All on the lily spray,
And she listeneth how to Jesus Christ
    The little children pray.
Lightly she spreads her friendly wings,
    And to Heaven's gate hath sped,
And unto the Father in heaven she bears
    The prayers which the children have said.

And back she comes from Heaven's gate,
    And brings — that dove so mild ! —
From the Father in heaven who hears her speak
    A blessing on every child.
Then children lift up a pious prayer, —
    It hears whatever you say,
That heavenly dove, so white and fair,
    All on the lily spray.

TRANS. BY MISS MARY HOWITT.

"COME UNTO ME."

As children once to Christ were brought,
    That he might bless them there,
So now we little children ought
    To seek the same by prayer.

And as so many years ago
    Poor babes his pity drew,
I'm sure he will not let me go
    Without a blessing too.

Then while, this favor to implore,
    My little hands are spread,
Do thou thy sacred blessing pour,
    Dear Jesus, on my head.

HYMNS FOR INFANT MINDS.

THE INFANT JESUS.

WHAT lovely infant can this be,
That in the little crib I see ?
So sweetly on the straw it lies,
It must have come from Paradise.

Who is that lady kneeling by,
And gazing on, so tenderly?
O, that is Mary, ever blest;
How full of joy her holy breast!

What man is that who seems to smile
And look so blissful all the while?
'T is holy Joseph, good and true;
The infant makes him happy too.

Who makes the crib so bright and dear?
What voices sing so sweetly here?
Ah! see, behind the window-pane,
The little angels looking in!

Who are these people kneeling down,
With crooked sticks, and hands so brown?
The shepherds; on the mountain-top
The little angels woke them up.

The ox and ass, how still and mild
They stand beside the holy child;
His little body underneath
They warm so kindly with their breath.

Hail, holy cave! though dark thou be,
The world is lighted up by thee,
Hail, holy Babe! creation stands
And moves upon thy little hands.

THE CHILDREN'S DESIRE.

I THINK, when I read the sweet story of old, —
    How when Jesus was here among men,
He once called little children as lambs to his fold, —
    I should like to have been with them then.
I wish that his hands had been placed on my head,
    That his arms had been thrown around me ;
And that I might have seen his kind look, when he said,
    " Let the little ones come unto me."

Yet still to his footstool in faith I may go,
    And there ask for a share of his love ;
And I know, if I earnestly seek him below,
    I shall see him and hear him above, —
In that beautiful place he has gone to prepare
    For all those who are washed and forgiven ;
And many dear children are gathering there,
    " For of such is the Kingdom of Heaven."

HYMN.

I WANT to be like Jesus,
    So lovely and so meek ;
For no one marked an angry word,
    That ever heard him speak.

I want to be like Jesus,
　For I never, never find
That he, though persecuted, was
　To any one unkind.

I want to be like Jesus,
　Engaged in doing good,
So that it may of me be said,
　" She hath done what she could."

Alas! I'm not like Jesus,
　As any one may see;
O gentle Saviour, send thy grace
　And make me like to thee!

MELODIES FOR CHILDHOOD.

CHRIST'S LOVE.

SEE the kind Shepherd, Jesus, stands,
　With all engaging charms;
Hark, how he calls the tender lambs,
　And folds them in his arms!

Permit them to approach, he cries,
　Nor scorn their humble name;
For 't was to bless such souls as these
　The Lord of angels came.

He'll lead us to the heavenly streams
  Where living waters flow,
And guide us to the fruitful fields
  Where trees of knowledge grow.

The feeblest lamb amidst the flock
  Shall be its Shepherd's care ;
While folded in the Saviour's arms,
  We're safe from every snare.

SUNDAY-SCHOOL HYMN-BOOK.

COME TO ME.

" LITTLE children, come to me ; "
  This is what the Saviour said ;
Little children, come and see
  Where those blessed words are read.

Thus ye hear the Saviour speak :
  " Come ye all, and learn of me,
I am gentle, lowly, meek ; "
  So should little children be.

When our Saviour from above
  From his Father did descend,
Taken in his arms of love,
  Children saw in him their friend.

Jesus little children blessed ;
  Blest in innocence they are ;
Little children, thus caressed,
  Praise him in your infant prayer !

FOLLEN.

LET THEM COME.

" LET them come, the little children,
  To my fold and to my breast,"
Said the gentle, loving Saviour,
  As the children round him pressed.

May we come, all false and sinning,
  With our passions all aglow ?
Did he welcome *thus* the children ?
  Would he meet and bless *us* so ?

He can help us in our passion,—
  Teach us how to turn away
From the power of each temptation
  That would lead our lives astray.

But to have his smile and favor,—
  To be called the Saviour's own,—
We must all be true and tender,
  Seeking, loving good alone.

Help us, help us, gentle Jesus!
　　We are very weak and small;
Stand between us and the evil;
　　Guide us through and over all.

We will struggle daily, hourly,
　　That we may by thee be blest:
To thy fold O let us enter!
　　Take us to thy loving breast.

A. S.

FORGIVENESS.

WHEN, for some little insult given,
　　My angry passions rise,
I 'll think how Jesus came from heaven,
　　And bore his injuries.

He was insulted every day,
　　Though all his words were kind;
But nothing men could do or say
　　Disturbed his heavenly mind.

Not all the wicked scoffs he heard,
　　Against the truths he taught,
Excited one reviling word,
　　Or one revengeful thought.

And when upon the cross he bled,
  With all his foes in view,
" Father, forgive their sins," he said ;
  " They know not what they do."

Dear Jesus, may I learn of thee
  My temper to amend ;
And speak the pardoning word for me,
  Whenever I offend.

JANE TAYLOR.

JESUS.

FEEBLE, helpless, how shall I
Learn to live, and learn to die ?
Who, O God ! my guide shall be ?
Who shall lead thy child to thee ?

Blessed Father, gracious one !
Thou hast sent thy holy Son ;
He will give the light I need,
He my trembling steps will lead.

Through this world, uncertain, dim,
Let me ever lean on him ;
From his precepts wisdom draw,
Make his life my solemn law.

7   J

Thus in deed, and thought, and word,
Led by Jesus Christ the Lord,
In my weakness, thus shall I
Learn to live, and learn to die ; —

Learn to live in peace and love,
Like the perfect ones above ;
Learn to die without a fear,
Feeling thee, my Father, near.

FURNESS.

"GIVE ME THY HEART."

HEAR ye not a voice from heaven,
To the listening spirit given ?
" Children, come ! " it seems to say,
" Give your hearts to me me to-day."

Sweet as is a mother's love,
Tender as the heavenly Dove,
Thus it speaks a Saviour's charms,
Thus it wins us to his arms.

Lord, may we remember thee,
While from pain and sorrow free ;
While our day is in its dew,
And the clouds of life are few.

Then, when night and age appear,
Thou wilt chase each doubt and fear;
Thou our glorious leader be,
When the stars shall fade and flee.

Now to thee, O Lord! we come,
In our morning's early bloom;
Breathe on us thy grace divine,
Touch our hearts, and make them thine.

Sunday-School Hymns.

SHEPHERD OF ISRAEL.

Shepherd of Israel, hear my prayer,
  And to my cry give heed;
Shepherd of Israel, lead me where
  Thy flocks in safety feed.

Whether upon the barren hills,
  Or on the desert bare,
Strike but thy rod, the purest rills
  And greenest herbs are there.

The shadow of a mighty rock
  Is in that weary land,
And heavenly dews fall on the flock
  Protected by thy hand.

The winds that blight, the wolves that slay,
  In vain their fury spend ;
Thy crook of love points out the way,
  Thy gracious arms defend.

Lead me, O lead me to thy fold !
  Earth has no rest beside ;
Shepherd of Israel, known of old,
  Be only thou my guide.

Whether the way be dark and drear,
  Or flowery, bright, and fair,
Shepherd of Israel, be thou near,
  And keep my footsteps there.

Whether where trees of Lebanon
  Or tents of Kedar rise,
Shepherd of Israel, lead me on —
  My home is in the skies.

SACRED OFFERING.

FOR A CHRISTIAN CHILD.

SEEING I am Jesus' lamb,
Ever glad at heart I am
O'er my Shepherd kind and good,
Who provides me daily food,
And his lamb by name doth call,
For he knows and loves us all.

Guided by his gentle staff
Where the sunny pastures laugh,
I go in and out and feed,
Lacking nothing that I need;
When I thirst, my feet he brings
To the fresh and living springs.

Must I not rejoice for this?
He is mine, and I am his;
And when these bright days are past,
Safely in his arms at last
He will bear me home to heaven;
Ah, what joy hath Jesus given!

LOUIS H. VON HAYM.

CHRISTMAS.

'T IS Christmas day! glad voices
　Repeat the pleasant sound;
And happy faces in our home,
　And loving looks, abound.
Why do we thus greet Christmas morn?
It is the day that Christ was born.

With little gifts that tell our love,
　With garlands on the wall,
With thankful hearts and helpful hands,
　We keep a festival.

Why do we thus keep Christmas morn?
It is the day that Christ was born.

Full eighteen hundred years ago
    Christ Jesus came on earth, —
He came, he lived, he died for us :
    We thank God for his birth ;
And therefore we keep Christmas morn,
The day our Saviour, Christ, was born.

And on this Christmas morning,
    When the frost is at the door,
Dear child ! in your warm, pleasant home,
    Think of the sick and poor :
So shall you well keep Christmas morn,
The day our Saviour, Christ, was born.

Christ healed the sick, and helped the poor,
    When he was on the earth :
Do what you can to be like him
    This morning of his birth ;
Help some one to keep Christmas morn,
The day your Saviour, Christ, was born.

HYMNS FOR YOUNG CHILDREN.

JESUS AND THE DOVE.

A CATHOLIC LEGEND.

With patient hand Jesus in clay once wrought,
  And made a snowy dove that upward flew:
Dear child, from all things draw some holy thought,
  That, like his dove, they may fly upward too.

MARY, the mother good and mild,
  Went forth one summer's day,
That Jesus and his comrades all
  In meadows green might play.

To find the brightest, freshest flowers,
  They search the meadows round,
They twined them all into a wreath,
  And little Jesus crowned.

Tired of play, they came at last
  And sat at Mary's feet,
While Jesus asked his mother dear
  A story to repeat.

" And we," said one, " from out this clay
  Will make some little birds,
So shall we all sit quietly
  And heed the mother's words."

Then Mary, in her gentle voice,
  Told of a little child,
Who lost her way one dark, dark night
  Upon a dreary wild ;

And how an angel came to her,
  And made all bright around,
And took the trembling little one
  From off the damp, hard ground ;

And how he bore her in his arms
  Up to the blue so far,
And how he laid her fast asleep,
  Down in a silver star.

The children sit at Mary's·feet,
  But not a word they say,
So busily their fingers work
  To mould the birds of clay.

But now the clay that Jesus held
  And turned unto the light,
And moulded with a patient touch,
  Changed to a perfect white.

And slowly grew within his hands
  A fair and gentle dove,
Whose eyes unclose, whose wings unfold,
  Beneath his look of love.

The children drop their birds of clay,
   And by his side they stand,
To look upon the wondrous dove
   He holds within his hand.

And when he bends and softly breathes,
   Wide are the wings outspread,
And when he bends and breathes again,
   It hovers round his head.

Slowly it rises in the air
   Before their eager eyes,
And with a white and steady wing,
   Higher and higher flies.

The children all stretch forth their arms,
   As if to draw it down :
" Dear Jesus made the little dove
   From out the clay so brown.

" Canst thou not live with us below,
   Thou little dove of clay,
And let us hold thee in our hands,
   And feed thee every day ?

" The little dove, it hears us not,
   But higher still doth fly ;
It could not live with us below,
   Its home is in the sky."

7 *

Mary, who silently saw all,
　That mother true and mild,
Folded her hands upon her breast,
　And kneeled before her child.

MARIA LOWELL.

NEW YEAR'S EVE.

The following stanzas are a translation, or rather adaptation, from a Swedish
tale, by ANDERSEN.

LITTLE Gretchen, little Gretchen,
　Wanders up and down the street,
The snow is on her yellow hair,
　The frost is at her feet.

The rows of long dark houses
　Without, look cold and damp,
By the struggling of the moonbeam,
　By the flicker of the lamp.

The clouds ride fast as horses,
　The wind is from the north,
But no one cares for Gretchen,
　And no one looketh forth.

Within those dark, damp houses
　Are merry faces bright,
And happy hearts are watching out
　The old year's latest night.

The board is spread with plenty,
  Where the smiling kindred meet ;
But the frost is on the pavement,
  And the beggars in the street.

With the little box of matches
  She could not sell all day,
And the thin, thin tattered mantle
  The wind blows every way.

She clingeth to the railing,
  She shivers in the gloom, —
There are parents sitting snugly
  By firelight in the room ;

And groups of busy children,
  Withdrawing just the tips
Of rosy fingers pressed in vain
  Against their burning lips,

With grave and earnest faces,
  Are whispering each other
Of presents for the new year, made
  For father or for mother.

But no one talks to Gretchen,
  And no one hears her speak,
No breath of little whisperers
  Comes warmly to her cheek ;

No little arms are round her,
　　Ah me! that there should be,
With so much happiness on earth,
　　So much of misery!

Sure they of many blessings
　　Should scatter blessings round,
As laden boughs in autumn fling
　　Their ripe fruits to the ground.

And the best love man can offer
　　To the God of love, be sure,
Is kindness to his little ones,
　　And bounty to his poor.

Little Gretchen, little Gretchen
　　Goes coldly on her way;
There's no one looketh out at her,
　　There's no one bids her stay.

Her home is cold and desolate,
　　No smile, no food, no fire,
But children clamorous for bread,
　　And an impatient sire.

So she sits down in an angle,
　　Where two great houses meet,
And she curleth up beneath her,
　　For warmth, her little feet.

And she looketh on the cold wall,
   And on the colder sky,
And wonders if the little stars
   Are bright fires up on high.

She heard a clock strike slowly,
   Up in a far church-tower,
With such a sad and solemn tone,
   Telling the midnight hour.

Then all the bells together
   Their merry music poured;
They were ringing in the feast,
   The circumcision of the Lord.

And she thought as she sat lonely,
   And listened to the chime,
Of wondrous things that she had loved
   To hear in the olden time.

And she remembered her of tales
   Her mother used to tell,
And of the cradle-songs she sang,
   When summer's twilight fell; —

Of good men and of angels,
   And of the Holy Child,
Who was cradled in a manger,
   When winter was most wild.

Who was poor, and cold, and hungry,
　And desolate and lone ;
And she thought the song had told
　He was ever with his own.

And all the poor and hungry,
　And forsaken ones are his :
" How good of him to look on me,
　In such a place as this."

Colder it grows and colder,
　But she does not feel it now,
For the pressure at her heart,
　And the weight upon her brow.

But she struck one little match
　On the wall so cold and bare,
That she might look around her,
　And see if He were there.

The single match has kindled,
　And by the light it threw,
It seemed to little Gretchen,
　The wall was rent in two.

And she could see the room within,
　The room all warm and bright,
With the fire-glow red, and dusky,
　And the tapers all alight.

And there were kindred gathered,
 Round the table richly spread,
With heaps of goodly viands,
 Red wine, and pleasant bread.

She could smell the fragrant savor,
 She could hear what they did say,
Then all was darkness once again,
 The match had burned away.

She struck another hastily,
 And now she seemed to see,
Within the same warm chamber,
 A glorious Christmas-tree.

The branches were all laden
 With such things as children prize, —
Bright gift for boy and maiden,
 She saw them with her eyes.

And she almost seemed to touch them,
 And to join the welcome shout;
When darkness fell around her,
 For the little match was out.

Another, yet another, she
 Has tried; they will not light,
Till all her little store she took,
 And struck with all her might.

And the whole miserable place
　　Was lighted with the glare,
.And lo! there hung a little child
　　Before her in the air.

There were blood-drops on his forehead,
　　And a spear-wound in his side,
And cruel nail-prints in his feet,
　　And in his hands spread wide.

And he looked upon her gently,
　　And she felt that he had known
Pain, hunger, cold, and sorrow,
　　Ay, equal to her own.

And he pointed to the laden board,
　　And to the Christmas-tree,
Then up to the cold sky, and said,
　　" Will Gretchen come with me ? "

The poor child felt her pulses fail,
　　She felt her eyeballs swim,
And a ringing sound was in her ears,
　　Like her dead mother's hymn.

And she folded both her thin white hands,
　　And turned from that bright board,
And from the golden gifts, and said,
　　" With thee, with thee, O Lord."

The chilly winter morning
  Breaks up in the dull skies,
On the city wrapt in vapor,
  On the spot where Gretchen lies.

The night was wild and stormy,
  The morn is cold and gray,
And good church-bells are ringing,
  Christ's circumcision day.

And holy men were praying
  In many a holy place ;
And little children's angels
  Sing songs before his face.

In her scant and tattered garment,
  With her back against the wall,
She sitteth cold and rigid,
  She answers not their call.

They have lifted her up fearfully,
  They shuddered as they said,
" It was a bitter, bitter night,
  The child is frozen dead."

The angels sang their greeting,
  For one more redeemed from sin ;
Men said, " It was a bitter night,
  Would no one let her in ? "

K

And they shuddered as they spoke of her,
And sighed : they could not see,
How much of happiness there was
With so much misery.

AN EASTERN LEGEND.

ONE evening Jesus lingered in the market-place,
Teaching the people parables of truth and grace,
When in the square remote a crowd was seen to rise,
And stop, with loathing gestures and abhorring cries.

The Master and his meek disciples went to see
What cause for this commotion and disgust could be,
And found a poor dead dog beside the gutter laid ;
Revolting sight ! at which each face its hate betrayed.

One held his nose, one shut his eyes, one turned away ;
And all among themselves began aloud to say :
" Detested creature ! " " He pollutes the earth and air ! "
" His eyes are blear ! " " His ears are foul ! " " His ribs
       are bare ! "

" In his torn hide there 's not a decent shoe-string left ! "
" No doubt the execrable cur was hung for theft ! "
Then Jesus spake, and dropped on him this saving
       wreath,
" Even pearls are dark before the whiteness of his teeth ! "

The pelting crowd grew silent and ashamed, like one
Rebuked by sight of wisdom higher than his own ;
And one exclaimed, " No creature so accursed can be,
But some good thing in him a loving eye will see."

ALGER'S EASTERN POETRY.

LOVE TO JESUS.

WHEN Jesus Christ was here below,
And spread his works of love abroad,
If I had lived as long ago,
I think I should have loved the Lord.

Jesus, who was so very kind,
Who came to pardon sinful men,
Who healed the sick, and cured the blind —
O, must I not have loved him then ?

But where is Jesus ? — is he dead ?
O no ! he lives in heaven above ;
" And blest are they," the Saviour said,
" Who, though they have not seen me, love."

JANE TAYLOR.

III. MORNING AND EVENING HYMNS.

THE GUARDIAN ANGEL.

DEAR Angel! ever at my side,
  How loving must thou be
To leave thy home in Heaven to guard
  A little child like me!

Thy beautiful and shining face
  I see not, though so near;
The sweetness of thy soft, low voice
  I am too deaf to hear.

I cannot feel thee touch my hand
  With pressure light and mild,
To check me, as my mother did
  When I was but a child.

But I have felt thee in my thoughts,
  Fighting with sin for me;
And when my heart loves God, I know
  The sweetness is from thee.

And when, dear Spirit, I kneel down
  Morning and night to prayer,
Something there is within my heart
  Which tells me thou art there.

Yes! when I pray, thou prayest too —
  Thy prayer is all for me;
And when I sleep, thou sleepest not,
  But watchest patiently.

Ah me! how lovely they must be
  Whom God has glorified;
Yet one of them, O sweetest thought!
  Is ever at my side.

And thou in life's last hour wilt bring
  A fresh supply of grace,
And afterwards wilt let me kiss
  Thy beautiful bright face.

Then for thy sake, dear Angel! now
  More humble will I be:
But I am weak, and when I fall,
  · O weary not for me;

But love me, love me, Angel dear!
  And I will love thee more;
And help me when my soul is cast
  Upon the eternal shore.

                              F. W. FABER.

BIRDS AND ANGELS.

HIGH the feathered warblers fly,
Singing in the clear blue sky;
Higher still the angels soar,
And sing in Heaven evermore.

Birds, come rest your wings awhile,
With me here the hours beguile;
Angels, downward turn your love,
Tell me of the joys above.

SONGS FROM THE GERMAN.

CHILD'S SONG.

FROM THE GERMAN.

WHEN at night I go to sleep,
 Fourteen angels are at hand; —
Two on my right their watches keep;
 Two on my left to bless me stand;
Two hover gently o'er my head;
Two guard the foot of my small bed;
Two wake me with the sun's first ray;
Two dress me nicely every day;
Two guide me on the heavenly road
That leads to Paradise and God.

MRS. FOLLEN.

THE ANGELS.

" WHERE are the angels, mother ?
　　·Though you have often said
They watched at night around me,
　　And safely kept my-bed ;

" Though every night I listen
　　Their voices low to hear,
Yet I have never heard them —
　　Where are they, mother dear ?

" And when the silver moonshine
　　Fills all my room with light,
And when the stars are shining,
　　So countless and so bright,

" I hope to see them coming,
　　With their fair forms, to me ;
Yet I have never seen them —
　　Mother, where can they be ?

" I saw a cloud, this evening,
　　Red with the setting sun ;
It was so very lovely,
　　I thought it might be one.

" But when it faded slowly,
  I knew it could not be,
For they are always shining —
  Why come they not to me ? "

" My child, when through your window
  Shines down the moonlight clear, —
When all is still and silent,
  And no kind friend is near, —

" Are you not glad and happy,
  And full of thoughts of love ?
Do you not think of heaven,
  That brighter land above ?

" These thoughts the angels bring you ;
  And though the gentle tone
Of their sweet voices comes not
  When you are all alone ;

" Yet they are always leaving,
  For earth, their homes on high ;
And though you cannot see them,
  You feel that they are nigh."

I WANT TO BE AN ANGEL.

I WANT to be an angel,
   And with the angels stand ;
A crown upon my forehead,
   And a harp within my hand.
Then, right before my Saviour,
   So glorious and so bright,
I 'd make the sweetest music,
   And praise him day and night.

I never should be weary,
   Nor ever shed a tear,
Nor ever know a sorrow,
   Nor ever feel a fear.
But, blessed, pure, and holy,
   I 'd dwell in Jesus' sight ;
And with ten thousand thousand,
   Praise him both day and night.

I know I 'm weak and sinful,
   But Jesus will forgive ;
For many little children
   Have gone to heaven to live.
Dear Saviour, when I languish,
   And lay me down to die,
O send a shining angel
   To bear me to the sky !

8

O, there I 'll be an angel,
    And with the angels stand;
A crown upon my forehead,
    A harp within my hand!
And there, before my Saviour,
    So glorious and so bright,
I 'll join the heavenly music
    And praise him day and night!

MELODIES FOR CHILDHOOD.

A CHILD'S PRAYER.

LORD, teach a little child to pray,
    And oh! accept my prayer;
Thou canst hear all the words I say,
    For thou art everywhere.

A little sparrow cannot fall
    Unnoticed, Lord, by thee;
And though I am so young and small,
    Thou dost take care of me.

Teach me to do whate'er is right,
    And when I sin, forgive;
And make it still my chief delight
    To serve thee while I live.

"BEAR EACH OTHER'S BURDENS."

HELP us to help each other, Lord,
  Each other's cross to bear ;
Let each his friendly aid afford,
  And feel his brother's care.

Help us to build each other up ;
  Our little stock improve ;
Increase our faith, confirm our hope,
  And perfect us in love.

Up into thee, our living Head,
  Let us in all things grow,
Till thou hast made us free indeed,
  And spotless here below.

THE LORD'S PRAYER.

OUR Father, who in heaven art,
  All hallowed be thy name !
Thy kingdom come, thy will be done
  In earth and heaven the same.

Give us this day our daily bread ;
  Our trespasses forgive,
As those who trespass against us
  Our pardon shall receive.

Into temptation lead us not,
   Deliver us from ill ;
For thine the kingdom, thine the power,
   And thine the glory still !

SACRED OFFERING.

THE SUN.

GET up, dear children, see ! the sun
His shining course has just begun !
So like a giant he comes forth
To run his course and light the earth.

Welcome, thrice welcome, lovely day !
Thou chasest darksome night away ;
O that our hearts, like thee, were bright
With Heaven's own purifying light !

GERMAN SONGS.

MORNING SONG.

WITH the dawn awaking,
   Lord, I sing thy praise ;
Guide me to thee, making
   Me to know thy ways.

All thy precepts keeping
   Whole and undefiled,
Waking, Lord, or sleeping,
   Let me be thy child.

IBID.

PRAYER.

WAKE, little child, the morn is gay,
　The air is fresh and cool ;
But pause awhile, and kneel to pray
Before you go to merry play,
　Before you go to school.

Kneel down and speak the holy words :
　God loves your simple prayer
Above the sweet songs of the birds,
The bleating of the gentle herds,
　The flowers that scent the air.

And when the quiet evenings come,
　And dew-drops wet the sod,
When bats and owls begin to roam,
And flocks and herds are driven home,
　Then kneel again to God.

Because you need him day and night,
　To shield you with his arm ;
To help you always to do right,
To feed your soul and give it light,
　And keep you safe from harm.

MELODIES FOR CHILDHOOD.

MORNING HYMN.

AWAKE, my soul, and with the sun
Thy daily stage of duty run ;
Shake off dull sloth, and joyful rise
To pay thy morning sacrifice.

Wake, and lift up thyself, my heart,
And with the angels bear thy part,
Who all night long unwearied sing
High praises to the Eternal King.

Glory to thee, who safe hast kept,
And hast refreshed me while I slept :
Grant, Lord, when I from death shall wake,
I may of endless life partake.

Lord, I to thee my vows renew ;
Dispel my sins as morning dew ;
Guard my first springs of thought and will,
And with thyself my spirit fill.

Direct, control, suggest, this day,
All I design, or do, or say,
That all my powers, with true delight,
To thy sole glory may unite.

BISHOP KENN.

MORNING HYMN.

O God! I thank thee that the night
    In·peace and rest hath passed away ;
And that I see, in this fair light,
    My Father's smile, which makes it day.

Be thou my Guide, and let me live
    As under thine all-seeing eye :
Supply my wants, my sins forgive,
    And make me happy when I die.

                                    Rev. J. Pierpont.

EVENING HYMN.

Another day its course hath run,
    And still, O God! thy child is blest ;
For thou hast been by day my sun,
    And thou wilt be by night my rest.

Sweet sleep descends, mine eyes to close ;
    And now, when all the world is still,
I give my body to repose,
    My spirit to my Father's will.

                                    Ibid

GOOD NIGHT.

THE sun is hidden from our sight,
   The birds are sleeping sound ;
'T is time to say to all, " Good night ! "
   And give a kiss all round.

Good night ! my father, mother, dear,
   Now kiss your little son ;
Good night ! my friends, both far and near,
   Good night to every one.

Good night ! ye merry, merry birds,
   Sleep well till morning light ;
Perhaps if you could sing in words,
   You would have said, " Good night ! "

To all my pretty flowers, good night !
   You blossom while I sleep ;
And all the stars, that shine so bright,
   With you their watches keep.

The moon is lighting up the skies,
   The stars are sparkling there ;
'T is time to shut our weary eyes,
   And say our evening prayer.

MRS. FOLLEN.

THE GOOD BOY'S HYMN ON GOING TO BED.

How sweet to lay my weary head
Upon my quiet little bed,
And feel assured, that all day long
I have not knowingly done wrong!

How sweet to hear my mother say,
"You have been very good to-day!"
How sweet to see my father's joy
When he can say, "My dear, good boy!"

How sweet it is my thoughts to send
To many a dear-loved distant friend,
And feel, if they my heart could see,
How very happy they would be!

How sweet to think that He whose love
Made all these shining worlds above,
My pure and happy heart can see,
And loves a little boy like me!

MRS. FOLLEN.

EVENING HYMN.

Now the sun hath gone so rest,
  Stars are coming faint and dim,
And the bird within his nest
  Sweetly sings his evening hymn.

8*   L

Have I tried mamma to mind?
Was I gentle in my play?
Have I been a true and kind,
Pleasant little girl to-day?

EVENING HYMN.

JESUS, tender Shepherd, hear me;
Bless thy little lamb to-night:
Through the darkness be thou near me,
Watch my sleep till morning light.

All this day thy hand has led me,
And I thank thee for thy care;
Thou hast clothed me, warmed, and fed me;
Listen to my evening prayer.

Let my sins be all forgiven,
Bless the friends I love so well;
Take me, when I die, to heaven,
Happy there with thee to dwell.

M. L. DUNCAN.

EVENING HYMN.

GOD has kept me, dearest mother,
Kindly, safely, through the day;

Let me thank him for his goodness,
  Ere the twilight fades away.

For my home and friends I thank him,
  For my father, mother, dear;
For the hills, the trees, the flowers,
  And the sky so bright and clear.

If I have been kind and gentle,
  If I 've spoken what was true,
Or if I 've been cross and selfish,
  He has seen and known it, too.

Those I love he will watch over,
  Though they may be far away,
For he loves good little children,
  And will hear the words they say.

EVENING HYMN.

Thou, from whom we never part,
  Thou, whose love is everywhere,
Thou, who seest every heart,
  Listen to our evening prayer.

Father! fill our souls with love, —
  Love unfailing, full, and free,
Love no injury can move,
  Love that ever rests on thee.

Heavenly Father ! through the night
   Keep us safe from every ill ;
Cheerful as the morning light,
   May we wake to do thy will.

Mrs. Follen.

EVENING HYMN.

Before I close my eyes to-night,
   Let me myself these questions ask :
Have I endeavored to do right,
   Nor thought my duty was a task ?

Have I been gentle, lowly, meek,
   And the small voice of conscience heard ?
When passion tempted me to speak,
   Have I repressed the angry word ?

Have I with cheerful zeal obeyed
   What my kind parents bid me do,
And not by word or action said
   The thing that was not strictly true ?

In hard temptation's troubled hour,
   Then have I stopped to think and pray,
That God would give my soul the power
   To chase the sinful thought away ?

O Thou who seest all my heart,
   Wilt thou forgive and love me still!
Wilt thou to me new strength impart,
   And make me love to do thy will!

Mrs. Follen.

EVENING HYMN.

GLORY to thee, my God! this night,
For all the blessings of the light:
Keep me, O keep me, King of kings,
Beneath the shadow of thy wings!

Forgive me, Lord, through thy dear Son,
The ills which I this day have done;
That with the world, myself, and thee,
I, ere I sleep, at peace may be.

Teach me to live, that I may dread
The grave as little as my bed;
Teach me to die, that so I may
Rise joyful at the judgment-day.

Be thou my guardian while I sleep;
Thy watchful station near me keep;
My heart with love celestial fill,
And guard me from the approach of ill.

Lord, let my heart forever share
The bliss of thy paternal care :
'T is heaven on earth, 't is heaven above,
To see thy face and sing thy love.

BISHOP KENN.

AN EVENING PRAYER.

LORD, thine eye is closéd never ;
   When night casts o'er earth her hood,
Thou remainest wakeful ever,
   And art like a shepherd good,
Who, through every darksome hour,
Tends his flock with watchful power.

   Grant, O Lord ! that we thy sheep
   May this night in safety sleep ;
   And when we again awake,
   Give us strength our cross to take ;
   And to order all our ways
   To thine honor and thy praise.

   Or, if thou hast willed that I
   Must before the morning die,
   Into thy hands to the end,
   Soul and body I commend.

Amen.
SONGS FROM THE GERMAN.

IV. MISCELLANEOUS.

WISDOM.

How happy is the child who hears
   Instruction's warning voice;
And who celestial wisdom makes
   His early, only choice.

Wisdom has treasures greater far
   Than east or west unfold;
And her rewards more precious are
   Than is the gain of gold.

She guides the young with innocence
   In pleasure's path to tread;
A crown of glory she bestows
   Upon the hoary head.

According as her labors rise,
   So her rewards increase;
Her ways are ways of pleasantness,
   And all her paths are peace.

THE HOLY CHILD.

By cool Siloam's shady rill
    How sweet the lily grows !
How sweet the breath, beneath the hill,
    Of Sharon's dewy rose !

Lo, such the child whose early feet
    The paths of peace have trod ;
Whose secret heart, with influence sweet,
    Is upward drawn to God !

O Thou, who giv'st us life and breath,
    We seek thy grace alone,
In childhood, manhood, age, and death,
    To keep us still thine own !

HEBER.

IMMORTAL BEAUTY.

Sweet day ! so cool, so calm, so bright,
    Bridal of earth and sky,
The dew shall weep thy fall to-night,
    For thou, alas ! must die.

Sweet rose ! in air whose odors wave,
    And color charms the eye,
Thy root is ever in its grave,
    And thou, alas ! must die.

Sweet Spring! of days and roses made,
  Whose charms for beauty vie,
Thy days depart, thy roses fade,
  Thou too, alas! must die.

Only a sweet and holy soul
  Hath tints that never fly;
While flowers decay, and seasons roll,
  This lives, and cannot die.

GEORGE HERBERT.

SUNDAY EVENING.

'T was night, and o'er the desert moor
  The wintry storm-gusts wildly blew,
And so we closed our cottage door
  And round our cheerful wood-fire drew:
Each joined the hymn of evening praise,
Then told a tale of Bible days.

First Charley, in his little chair,
  With sober face, his tale began,
And told us of the faith and prayer
  Of Daniel in the lion's den;
And how the lions were afraid
To kill the righteous man who prayed.

Then Henry spoke of Israel's guide, —
  The cloud by day, the fire by night,

And said, whatever might betide,
    To trust in God is always right ;
For he is still, to those who pray,
A fire by night, a cloud by day.

 ·And little Freddy told of three
    Who once a fiery furnace trod,
Because they would not bow the knee
    In worship to an idol-god ;
And how, to save them from the flame,
The Son of God in glory came.

Then little Susan told of One
    Who kindly all our sorrows bore —
Though rich in heaven, on earth became
    For us so very, very poor,
That, though the foxes had a bed,
He had not where to lay his head.

The tale was told, — a crystal tear
    Rose brightly to each sparkling eye,
And then in accents soft and clear
    Our evening hymn again rolled high ;
Each little girl, each little boy
Joined in the strains of solemn joy.

Then grandpa prayed, — that dear old man,
    With wrinkled brow and hoary hair,
While all the little children ran
    To kneel around his elbow-chair.

And thus the Sunday evening passed,
In peace and pleasure to the last.

CHOICE POEMS.

THE TEN COMMANDMENTS.

EXODUS, CHAP. XX.

1. THOU shalt have no more gods but me ;
2. Before no idol bow thy knee.
3. Take not the name of God in vain,
4. Nor dare the Sabbath day profane.
5. Give both thy parents honor due :
6. Take heed that thou no murder do.
7. Abstain from words and deeds unclean,
8. Nor steal though thou art poor and mean,
9. Nor make a wilful lie, nor love it.
10. What is thy neighbor's dare not covet.

THE DELUGE.

A RAIN once fell upon the earth
  For many a day and night,
And hid the flowers, the grass, the trees,
  The birds and beasts, from sight.

The deep waves covered all the land,
  And mountain-tops so high ;

And nothing could be seen around,
 But water, and the sky.

But yet there was one moving thing, —
 A still and lonely ark, —
That many a weary day and night
 Sailed o'er that ocean dark.

At last, a little dove was forth
 From that lone vessel sent ;
But, wearied, to the ark again,
 When evening came, she bent.

Again she went, but soon returned,
 And in her beak was seen
A little twig — an olive-branch —
 With leaves of shining green.

The waters sank, and then the dove
 Flew from the ark once more,
And came not back, but lived among
 The tree-tops, as before.

Then from the ark they all came forth,
 With songs of joy and praise ;
And once again the green earth smiled
 Beneath the sun's warm rays.

THE ARK AND DOVE.

THERE was a noble ark,
Sailing o'er waters dark
   And wild around ;
Not one tall tree was seen,
Nor flower, nor leaf of green —
   All, all was drowned.

Then a soft wing was spread,
And o'er the billows dread
   A meek dove flew ;
But on that shoreless tide,
No living thing she spied
   To cheer her view.

So to the ark she fled,
With weary, drooping head,
   To seek for rest :
Christ is thy ark, my love,
Thou art the tender dove ;
   Fly to his breast.

MRS. SIGOURNEY.

THE STORY OF MOSES.

" TELL me a Sunday story,"
   A dear child said to me ;

And I bent down and kissed her
　And placed her on my knee.

" Once, long ago, in countries
　Far, very far away,
Where the cold snow-storm never comes,
　And all is bright and gay,

" There lived a king, so cruel,
　He gave this stern command,
That all the little children
　Must die, throughout the land.

" But still there was one mother
　Who kept her baby dear,
And quickly hushed its crying,
　In silence and in fear ;

" But when she could no longer
　Her precious baby hide,
She did not like to throw him
　Upon the rushing tide ;

" And so a little basket
　She made, of rushes stout,
And plastered it with clay and pitch
　To keep the water out.

" Then in this basket-cradle
　She put the little child ;

And quietly he floated down
  Among the rushes wild.

" Just then the king's own daughter
  Came to the water's edge,
And saw the basket floating
  Among the grass and sedge.

" She drew it from the water,
  And called the babe her own,
And kept him till to be a man
  That little boy had grown.

" And when you read the Bible, —
  Which you will learn to do, —
You 'll see how great and good he was,
  And how God loved him, too."

DAVID IN THE CAVE OF ADULLAM.

DAVID and his three captains bold
Kept ambush once within a hold.
It was Adullam's cave,
Nigh which no water they could have,
Nor spring, nor running brook was near
To quench the thirst that parched them there.
Then David, king of Israel,
Straight bethought him of a well,

Which stood beside the city gate,
At Bethle'm ; where, before his state
Of kingly dignity, he had
Oft drunk his fill, a shepherd lad ;
But now his fierce Philistine foe
Encamped before it he does know.
Yet ne'er the less, with heat opprest,
Those three bold captains he addrest ;
And wished that one to him would bring
Some water from his native spring.
His valiant captains instantly
To execute his will did fly.
The mighty three the ranks broke through
Of arméd foes, and water drew
For David, their beloved king,
At his own sweet, native spring.
Back through their arméd foes they haste,
With the hard-earned treasure graced.
But when the good king David found
What they had done, he on the ground
The water poured.   " Because," said he,
" That it was at the jeopardy
Of your three lives this thing ye did,
That I should drink it, God forbid."

CHARLES LAMB.

HERODIAS'S DAUGHTER.

ONCE on a charger there was laid,
And brought before a royal maid,
As price of attitude and grace,
A guiltless head, a holy face.

It was on Herod's natal day,
Who o'er Judæa's land held sway.
He married his own brother's wife,
Wicked Herodias. She the life
Of John the Baptist long had sought,
Because he openly had taught
That she a life unlawful led,
Having her husband's brother wed.

This was he, that saintly John,
Who in the wilderness alone
Abiding, did for clothing wear
A garment made of camel's-hair;
Honey and locusts were his food,
And he was most severely good.
He preachéd penitence and tears,
And waking first the sinner's fears,
Prepared a path, made smooth a way,
For his diviner Master's day.

Herod kept in princely state
His birthday. On his throne he sate,

9   M

After the feast, beholding her
Who danced with grace peculiar;
Fair Salomé, who did excel
All in that land for dancing well.
The feastful monarch's heart was fired,
And whatsoe'er thing she desired,
Though half his kingdom it should be,
He in his pleasure swore that he
Would give the graceful Salomé.
The damsel was Herodias' daughter.
She to the queen hastes, and besought her
To teach her what great gift to name.
Instructed by Herodias, came
The damsel back; to Herod said,
" Give me John the Baptist's head;
And in a charger let it be
Hither straightway brought to me."
Herod her suit would fain deny,
But for his oath's sake must comply.

When painters would by art express
Beauty in unloveliness,
They, Herodias' daughter, thee
The fittest subject take to be.
They give thy form and features grace;
But ever in thy beauteous face
They show a steadfast, cruel gaze,
An eye unpitying; and amaze
In all beholders deep they mark,
That thou betrayest not one spark

Of feeling for the ruthless deed,
That did thy praiseful dance succeed.
For on the head they make you look,
As if a sullen joy you took
A cruel triumph, wicked pride,
That for your sport a saint had died.

CHARLES LAMB.

THE SPARTAN BOY.

WHEN I the memory repeat
Of the heroic actions great,
Which, in contempt of pain and death,
Were done by men who drew their breath
In ages past, I find no deed
That can in fortitude exceed
The noble boy, in Sparta bred,
Who in the temple ministered.
By the sacrifice he stands,
The lighted incense in his hands;
Through the smoking censer's lid
Dropped a burning coal, which slid
Into his sleeve, and passéd in
Between the folds, e'en to the skin.
Dire was the pain which then he proved;
But not for this his sleeve he moved,
Or would the scorching ember shake
Out from the folds, lest it should make
Any confusion, or excite
Disturbance at the sacred rite;

But close he kept the burning coal,
Till it eat itself a hole
In his flesh. The standers by
Saw no sign and heard no cry.
All this he did in noble scorn,
And for he was a Spartan born.

In this story thou mayest see
That may useful prove to thee.
By this example thou wilt find,
That, to the ingenuous mind,
Shame can greater anguish bring
Than the body's suffering ;
That pain is not the worst of ills, —
Not when it the body kills ;
That in fair Religion's cause,
For thy country, or the laws,
When occasion dire shall offer,
'T is reproachful not to suffer.

MARY LAMB.

ABOU-BEN-ADHEM.

ABOU-BEN-ADHEM — may his tribe increase ! —
Awoke one night from a deep dream of peace,
And saw, within the moonlight of his room,
Making it rich and like a lily's bloom,
An angel writing in a book of gold.
Exceeding peace had made Ben-Adhem bold ;

And to the Presence in the room he said,
" What writest thou ? " The vision raised his head,
And, with a look made of all sweet accord,
Answered, " The names of those who love the Lord."
" And is mine one ? " said Abou. " Nay, not so,"
Replied the angel. Abou spake more low,
But cheerily still ; and said, " I pray thee, then,
Write me as one that loves his fellow-men."
The angel wrote, and vanished. The next night
He came again, with a great wakening light,
And showed the names whom love of God had blest ;
And, lo ! Ben-Adhem's name led all the rest !

LEIGH HUNT.

THE HEART A BELL.

YOUR heart is beating day by day :
If it could speak, what would it say ?
The hours of night its pulses tell ; —
Have you, my child, considered well
What means this restless little heart,
That doth so well perform its part ?

It is a little bell, whose tone
Is heard by you and God alone.
At your soul's door it hangs ; and there
His Spirit stays with loving care,
And rings the bell, and deigns to wait
To see if closed remains the gate.

He rings and waits.   O then begin
At once your prayer, " Lord, enter in ! "

So when its time on earth is past,
Your heart will beat no more at last ;
And when its latest pulse is o'er,
'T will go and knock at Heaven's door ;
And stand without, and patient wait,
To see if Christ will ope the gate,
And say : " Here endless joys begin,
Here, faithful servant, enter in !
I was on earth thy cherished guest,
And now in Heaven I give thee rest.
Receive at length thy due reward ;
Enjoy the blessings of thy Lord."

SONGS FROM THE GERMAN.

PROFANITY.

TAKE not God's name in vain ;
   Speak not that holy name, —
Not with a laughing lip,
   Not in thy playful game ;
For the great God of all
   Heareth each word we say :
He will remember it,
   In the great judgment-day.

Hush! for his hosts, unseen,
 Are watching over thee;
His angels spread their wings,
 Thy shelter kind to be.
Wilt thou, with words profane,
 Rash and undutiful,
Scatter thine angel-guards,
 Glorious and beautiful?

Honor God's holy name:
 Speak it with thought and care;
Sing it in holy hymns;
 Breathe it in earnest prayer.
But not with sudden cry,
 In thy light joy or pain:
God will hold guilty all
 Who take his name in vain!

SUNDAY-SCHOOL HYMNS.

CONSCIENCE.

WHEN a foolish thought within
 Tries to take us in a snare,
Conscience tells us, "It is sin,"
 And entreats us to beware.

If in something we transgress,
 And are tempted to deny,

Conscience says, " Your fault confess ;
   Do not dare to tell a lie."

In the morning when we rise,
   And would fain omit to pray,
" Child, consider," Conscience cries ;
   " Should not God be sought to-day ? "

When, within His holy walls,
   Far abroad our thoughts we send,
Conscience often loudly calls,
   And entreats us to attend.

When our angry passions rise,
   Tempting to revenge an ill ;
" Now subdue it," Conscience cries ;
   " Do command your temper still."

Thus, without our will or choice,
   This good monitor within,
With a secret warning voice,
   Tells us to beware of sin.

But if we should disregard
   While this friendly voice would call,
Conscience soon will grow so hard
   That it will not speak at all.

                HYMNS FOR INFANT MINDS.

THE UNSEEN.

THE wind blows down the largest tree,
And yet the wind I cannot see.
Playmates far off, that have been kind,
My thought can bring before my mind ;
The past by it is present brought,
And yet I cannot see my thought.
The charming rose perfumes the air,
Yet I can see no perfumes there.
Blithe robin's notes — how sweet, how clear,
From his small bill they reach my ear !
And whilst upon the air they float,
I hear, yet cannot see a note.
When I would do what is forbid,
By something in my heart I'm chid ;
When good I think, then quick and pat
The something says, " My child, do that."
When I too near the stream would go,
So pleased to see the waters flow,
That something says, without a sound,
" Take care, dear child ! you may be drowned."
And for the poor whene'er I grieve,
That something says, " A penny give."
Thus spirits good and ill there be,
Although invisible to me :
Whate'er I do, they see me still.
Then, O good Spirits ! guide my will.

ADELAIDE TAYLOR.

9 *

ETERNITY.

How long sometimes a day appears !
    And weeks, how long are they !
Months move as slow as if the years
    Would never pass away.

But even years are fleeting by,
    And soon must all be gone ;
For day by day, as minutes fly,
    Eternity comes on.

Days, months, and years must have an end :
    Eternity has none !
'T will always have as long to spend
    As when it first begun.

Great God ! although we cannot tell
    How such a thing can be,
We humbly pray that we may dwell
    That long, long time with thee.

JANE TAYLOR.

IMMORTALITY.

YON butterfly, whose airy form
    Flits o'er the garden-wall,

Was once a little crawling worm,
  And could not fly at all.

The little worm was then enclosed
  Within a shell-like case,
And there it quietly reposed
  Until its change took place.

And now on red and purple wings
  It roves, as free as air,
Visiting all the lovely things
  That make the earth so fair.

And we — if humbly we behave,
  And do the will of God,
And strive to follow, to our grave,
  The paths the saints have trod —

Shall find a change more glorious far
  Than that which came to light,
When, bursting through its prison bar,
  The butterfly took flight.

Through Christ, who reigns above the skies,
  To us it will be given
Aloft on angels' wings to rise,
  And taste the joys of heaven.

SONGS FROM THE GERMAN.

THE STARS.

"STARS, that on your wondrous way
   Travel through the evening sky,
Is there nothing you can say
   To a child so small as I ?
Tell me — for I long to know —
Who has made you sparkle so ?"

" Child, as truly as we roll
   Through the dark and distant sky,
You have an immortal soul,
   Born to live when we shall die :
Suns and planets pass away,
Spirits never can decay.

" When, some thousand years at most,
   All their little time have spent,
One by one our sparkling host
   Shall forsake the firmament,
We shall from our glory fall ;
You must live beyond us all.

" Yes, and God, who bade us roll,
   God, who hung us in the sky,
Stoops to watch an infant's soul,
   With a condescending eye,
And esteems it dearer far,
More in value than a star !

"O then, while your breath is given,
  Pour it out in fervent prayer,
And beseech the God of Heaven
  To receive your spirit there;
As a living star to blaze
Ever to your Saviour's praise."

HYMNS FOR INFANT MINDS.

A CHRISTMAS HYMN.

IT was the calm and silent night!
  Seven hundred years and fifty-three
Had Rome been growing up to might,
  And now was queen of land and sea!
No sound was heard of clashing wars,
  Peace brooded o'er the hushed domain;
Apollo, Pallas, Jove, and Mars
  Held undisturbed their ancient reign, —
      In the solemn midnight,
          Centuries ago!

'T was in the calm and silent night!
  The senator of haughty Rome
Impatient urged his chariot's flight,
  From lordly revel rolling home.
Triumphal arches, gleaming, swell
  His breast with thoughts of boundless sway:

What recked the Roman what befell
  A paltry province far away, —
    In the solemn midnight,
      Centuries ago ?

Within that province far away
  Went plodding home a weary boor ;
A streak of light before him lay,
  Fallen through a half-shut stable door
Across his path.   He paused, for naught
  Told what was going on within :
How keen the stars, his only thought ;
  The air how calm, and cold, and thin, —
    In the solemn midnight,
      Centuries ago !

O strange indifference ! — low and high
  Drowsed over common joys and cares ;
The earth was still, but knew not why :
  The world was listening — unawares !
How calm a moment may precede
  One that shall thrill the world forever !
To that still moment none would heed,
  Man's doom was linked, no more to sever, —
    In the solemn midnight,
      Centuries ago !

It is the calm and silent night !
  A thousand bells ring out, and throw
Their joyous peals abroad, and smite
  The darkness, charmed and holy now !

The night that erst no shame had worn,
　To it a happy name is given;
For in that stable lay, new-born,
　The peaceful Prince of earth and heaven, —
　　In the solemn midnight,
　　　Centuries ago!

ALFRED DORNETT.

FOREST SCENE IN THE DAYS OF WICKLIFF.

A LITTLE child, she read a book,
　Beside an open door;
And as she read page after page,
　She wondered more and more.

Her little finger, carefully,
　Went pointing out the place;
Her golden locks hung drooping down,
　And shadowed half her face.

The open book lay on her knee,
　Her eyes on it were bent;
And as she read page after page,
　Her color came and went.

She sat upon a mossy stone,
　An open door beside;
And round, for miles on every side,
　Stretched out a forest wide.

The summer sun shone on the trees, —
  The deer lay in the shade;
And overhead the singing-birds
  Their pleasant clamor made.

There was no garden round the house,
  And it was low and small;
The forest sward grew to the door,
  The lichens on the wall.

There was no garden round about,
  Yet flowers were growing free;
The cowslip and the daffodil
  Upon the forest lea.

The butterfly went flitting by;
  The bees were in the flowers;
But the little child sat steadfastly,
  As she had sat for hours.

" Why sit ye here, my little maid ? "
  An aged pilgrim spake;
The child looked upward from her book
  Like one but just awake.

Back fell her locks of golden hair,
  And solemn was her look;
And thus she answered, witlessly,
  " O sir, I read this book ! "

" And what is there within that book
　To win a child like thee ?
Up ! join thy mates, the singing-birds,
　And frolic with the bee."

" Nay, sir, I cannot leave the book,
　I love it more than play ;
I 've read all legends, but this one
　Ne'er saw I till to-day.

" And there is something in this book
　That makes all care begone ;
And yet I weep, I know not why,
　As I go reading on."

" Who art thou, child, that thou shouldst read
　A book with mickle heed ?
Books are for clerks ; — the king himself
　Hath much ado — to read."

" My father is a forester,
　A bowman keen and good ;
He keeps the deer within their bounds,
　And worketh in the wood.

" My mother died at Candlemas ; —
　The flowers are all in blow
Upon her grave, at Allenby,
　Down in the vale below."

N

This said, unto her book she turned,
    As steadfast as before ; —
" Nay," said the pilgrim, " nay, not yet,
    And you must tell me more.

" Who was it taught you thus to read ? "
    " Ah, sir ! it was my mother ;
She taught me both to read and spell,
    And so she taught my brother.

" My brother dwelt at Allenby,
    With the good monk alway ;
And this new book he brought to me,
    But only for one day.

" O, sir, it is a wondrous book,
    Better than Charlemagne ;
And be you pleased to leave me now,
    I 'll read in it again."

" Nay, read to me," the pilgrim said ;
    And the little child went on
To read of Christ, as is set forth
    In the Gospel of St. John.

On, on she read, and gentle tears
    Adown her cheeks did glide ;
The pilgrim sat with bended head,
    And he wept by her side.

"I've heard," said he, "the Archbishop, —
   I've heard the Pope, at Rome, —
But never did their spoken words
   Thus to my spirit come.

"The book, it is a blessed book,
   Its name, what may it be?"
Said she, "They are the words of Christ
   That I have read to thee,
Now done into the English tongue,
   For folks unlearned as me."

"Give me the book, and let me read, —
   My soul is strangely stirred;
They are such words of love and truth
   As I ne'er before have heard."

The little girl gave up the book,
   And the pilgrim, old and brown,
With reverend lips did kiss the page,
   Then on the stone sat down.

And aye he read page after page,
   Page after page he turned;
And as he read their blessed words,
   His heart within him burned.

Still, still the book the old man read,
   As he would ne'er have done;
From the hour of noon he read the book
   Until the set of sun.

The little child, she brought him out
 A cake of wheaten bread;
And it lay unbroken at eventide,
 Nor did he raise his head.

Then came the sturdy forester
 Along the homeward track,
Whistling aloud a hunting tune,
 With a slain deer on his back.

Loud greeting gave the forester
 Unto the pilgrim poor, —
The old man rose with thoughtful brow,
 And entered at the door.

They two, they sat them down to meat,
 And the pilgrim 'gan to tell
How he had eaten on Olivet,
 And drank at Jacob's well.

And then he told him he had knelt
 Where'er our Lord had prayed,
How he had in the garden been,
 And the tomb where He was laid.

And then he turned unto the book,
 And read in English plain,
How Christ had died on Calvary,
 How he had risen again.

As water to the parchéd soil,
  As to the hungry, bread,
So fell upon the woodman's soul
  Each word the pilgrim read.

Thus, through the midnight did they read,
  Until the dawn of day ;
And then came in the woodman's son,
  To fetch the book away.

All quick and troubled was his speech, —
  His face was pale with dread ;
For he said the king had made a law
  That the book should not be read ;
For it was such a fearful heresy,
  The holy Abbot said.

                            MARY HOWITT.

PART V.

OLDER CHILDREN.

THE SPRING-TIME OF LIFE.

FROM "WILLIE WINKIE."

THE summer comes with rosy wreaths,
   To dance among the fragrant flowers,
While friendly autumn plenty breathes,
   And blessings in abundant showers.
E'en winter with its frost and snow
   Brings much the mind to calm and cheer,
But there 's a season worth them all
   And that 's the spring-time of the year.

In spring the farmer ploughs the field
    That yet will wave with yellow corn,
In spring the birdie builds its nest
    In foggy bank or budding thorn ;
The bank and brae, the hill and dell,
    A song of hope are heard to sing,
And summer, autumn, winter tell
    With joy and grief the work of spring.

Now youth 's the spring-time of your life,
    When seed is sown with care and toil,
And hopes are high and fears are rife,
    Lest weeds should rise the grain to spoil.
I 've sown the seed, my bairnies dear,
    By precept and example too,
And may the Hand that guides us here
    Preserve us all the journey through.

But soon the time will come when you
    May lose a mother's tender care,
A world with sorrows not a few,
    With all its stormy strife to share :
Then as you pass through life along
    Let fortune kind or frowning prove,
Ne'er let the Tempter lead you wrong,
    But still be guided by His love.

GEORGE DONALD.

THE PURPOSE OF LIFE.

HAST thou, midst life's empty noises,
 Heard the solemn steps of Time,
And the low, mysterious voices
 Of another clime ?

Early hath life's mighty question
 Thrilled within thy heart of youth,
With a deep and strong beseeching, —
 What, and where, is truth ?

Not to ease and aimless quiet
 Doth the inward answer tend ;
But to works of love and duty,
 As our being's end.

Earnest toil and strong endeavor
 Of a spirit which within
Wrestles with familiar evil
 And besetting sin ;

And without, with tireless vigor,
 Steady heart, and purpose strong,
In the power of Truth assaileth
 Every form of wrong.

J. G. WHITTIER.

THE BUILDING OF THE HOUSE.

I HAVE a wondrous house to build,
  A dwelling, humble yet divine ;
A lowly cottage to be filled
  With all the jewels of the mine.
How shall I build it strong and fair, —
This noble house, this lodging rare,
  So small and modest, yet so great ?
How shall I fill its chambers bare
  With use, with ornaments, with state ?

My God hath given the stone and clay ;
  'T is I must fashion them aright ;
'T is I must mould them day by day,
  And make my labor my delight ;
This cot, this palace, this fair home,
This pleasure-house, this holy dome,
  Must be in all proportions fit,
That heavenly messengers may come
  To lodge with him who tenants it.

No fairy bower this house must be,
  To totter at each gale that starts,
But of substantial masonry,
  Symmetrical in all its parts :
Fit in its strength to stand sublime

For seventy years of mortal time,
   Defiant of the storm and rain,
And well attempered to the clime
   In every cranny, nook, and pane.

I 'll build it so, that if the blast
   Around it whistle loud and long,
The tempest when its rage has passed
   Shall leave its rafters doubly strong.
I 'll build it so that travellers by
Shall view it with admiring eye,
   For its commodiousness and grace :
Firm on the ground, — straight to the sky, —
   A meek, but goodly dwelling-place.

Thus noble in its outward form,
   Within I 'll build it clean and white ;
Not cheerless cold, but happy warm,
   And ever open to the light.
No tortuous passages or stair,
No chamber foul, or dungeon lair,
   No gloomy attic, shall there be,
But wide apartments, ordered fair,
   And redolent of purity.

With three compartments furnished well,
   The house shall be a home complete ;
Wherein, should circumstance rebel,
   The humble tenant may retreat.
The first, a room wherein to deal

With men for human nature's weal,
  A room where he may work or play,
And all his social life reveal
  In its pure texture, day by day.

The second for his wisdom sought,
  Where, with his chosen book or friend,
He may employ his active thought
  To virtuous or exalted end.
A chamber lofty and serene,
With a door-window to the green,
  Smooth-shaven sward, and arching bowers,
Where love, or talk, or song between
  May gild his intellectual hours.

The third an oratory dim,
  But beautiful, where he may raise,
Unheard of men, his daily hymn
  Of love and gratitude and praise ;
Where he may revel in the light
Of things unseen and infinite,
  And learn how little he may be,
And yet how awful in thy sight,
  Ineffable Eternity !

Such is the house that I must build ;
  This is the cottage, this the dome,
And this the palace, treasure filled,
  For an immortal's earthly home.
O noble work of toil and care !

O task most difficult and rare !
　O simple but most arduous plan !
To raise a dwelling-place so fair,
　The sanctuary of a Man.

CHAS. MACKAY.

THE SCULPTOR BOY.

CHISEL in hand stood a sculptor boy,
　With his marble block before him ;
And his face lit up, with a smile of joy,
　As an angel-dream passed o'er him :
He carved it then on the yielding stone,
　With many a sharp incision ;
With Heaven's own light the sculpture shone :
　He had caught that angel-vision.

Sculptors of life are we, as we stand,
　With our souls, uncarved, before us,
Waiting the hour when, at God's command,
　Our life-dream shall pass o'er us.
If we carve it then, on the yielding stone,
　With many a sharp incision,
Its heavenly beauty shall be our own,
　Our lives, that angel-vision.

BISHOP DOANE.

A PSALM OF LIFE.

TELL me not, in mournful numbers,
    Life is but an empty dream!
For the soul is dead that slumbers,
    And things are not what they seem.

Life is real! Life is earnest!
    And the grave is not its goal:
Dust thou art, to dust returnest,
    Was not spoken of the soul.

Not enjoyment, and not sorrow,
    Is our destined end or way;
But to act, that each to-morrow
    Find us farther than to-day.

Art is long, and Time is fleeting,
    And our hearts, though stout and brave,
Still, like muffled drums, are beating
    Funeral marches to the grave.

In the world's broad field of battle
    In the bivouac of Life,
Be not like dumb, driven cattle!
    Be a hero in the strife!

Trust no Future, howe'er pleasant!
    Let the dead Past bury its dead!

Act, — act in the living Present!
　　Heart within, and God o'erhead!

Lives of great men all remind us
　　We can make our lives sublime,
And, departing, leave behind us
　　Footprints on the sands of time;

Footprints, that perhaps another,
　　Sailing o'er life's solemn main,
A forlorn and shipwrecked brother,
　　Seeing, shall take heart again.

Let us, then, be up and doing,
　　With a heart for any fate;
Still achieving, still pursuing,
　　Learn to labor and to wait.

LONGFELLOW.

LABOR.

PAUSE not to dream of the future before us:
Pause not to weep the wild cares that come o'er us:
Hark, how Creation's deep, musical chorus
　　Unintermitting, goes up into Heaven!
Never the ocean wave falters in flowing:
Never the little seed stops in its growing;
More and more richly the Rose-heart keeps glowing,
　　Till from its nourishing stem it is riven.

" Labor is worship ! " — the robin is singing ;
" Labor is worship ! " — the wild bee is ringing :
Listen that eloquent whisper unspringing
   Speaks to my soul from out nature's great heart,
From the dark cloud flows the life-giving shower ;
From the rough sod blows the soft-breathing flower ;
From the small insect, the rich coral bower ;
   Only man, in the plan, shrinks from his part.

Labor is life ! — 'T is the still water faileth ;
Idleness ever despaireth, bewaileth ;
Keep the watch wound, for the dark rust assaileth !
   Flowers droop and die in the stillness of noon.
Labor is glory ! the flying cloud lightens ;
Only the waving wing changes and brightens ;
Idle hearts only the dark future frightens :
   Play the sweet keys, wouldst thou keep them in tune !

Labor is rest from the sorrows that greet us ;
Rest from all petty vexations that meet us,
Rest from sin-promptings that ever entreat us,
   Rest from world-sirens that lure us to ill.
Work — and pure slumbers shall wait on thy pillow ;
Work — thou shalt ride over Care's coming billow ;
Lie not down wearied 'neath Woe's weeping willow !
   Work with a stout heart and resolute will !

Droop not tho' shame, sin, and anguish are round thee !
Bravely fling off the cold chain that hath bound thee !
Look to yon pure Heaven smiling beyond thee !

Rest not content in thy darkness — a clod !
Work — for some good, — be it ever so slowly !
Cherish some flower, — be it ever so lowly !
Labor ! All labor is noble and holy :
Let thy great deeds be thy prayer to thy God !

MRS. F. S. OSGOOD.

TRUE HAPPINESS.

How happy is he born and taught
 That serveth not another's will,
Whose armor is his honest thought,
 And simple truth his utmost skill !

Whose passions not his masters are,
 Whose soul is still prepared for death,
Untied unto the world by care
 Of public fame or private breath ; —

Who hath his life from rumors freed ;
 Whose conscience is his strong retreat ;
Whose state can neither flatterers feed,
 Nor ruin make oppressors great ; —

Who God doth late and early pray
 More of his grace than gifts to lend,
And walks with man from day to day,
 As with a brother and a friend.

This man is freed from servile bands
  Of hope to rise, or fear to fall ;
Lord of himself, though not of lands,
  And, having nothing, yet hath all.

SIR H. WOTTON.

FREEDOM.

Is true Freedom but to break
Fetters for our own dear sake,
And, with leathern hearts, forget
That we owe mankind a debt ?
No ! true freedom is to share
All the chains our brothers wear,
And, with heart and hand, to be
Earnest to make others free !

They are slaves who fear to speak
For the fallen and the weak ;
They are slaves who will not choose
Hatred, scoffing, and abuse,
Rather than in silence shrink
From the truth they needs must think ;
They are slaves who dare not be
In the right with two or three.

J. R. LOWELL.

THE HERITAGE.

THE rich man's son inherits lands,
  And piles of brick, and stone, and gold,
And he inherits soft white hands,
  And tender flesh that fears the cold,
  Nor dares to wear a garment old ;
A heritage, it seems to me,
One scarce would wish to hold in fee.

The rich man's son inherits cares ;
  The bank may break, the factory burn,
A breath may burst his bubble shares,
  And soft white hands could hardly earn
  A living that would serve his turn ;
A heritage, it seems to me,
One scarce would wish to hold in fee.

The rich man's son inherits wants,
  His stomach craves for dainty fare ;
With sated heart, he hears the pants
  Of toiling hinds with brown arms bare,
  And wearies in his easy-chair ;
A heritage, it seems to me,
One scarce would wish to hold in fee.

What doth the poor man's son inherit ?
  Wishes o'erjoyed with humble things,

A rank adjudged by toil-won merit,
   Content that from employment springs,
   A heart that in his labor sings;
A heritage, it seems to me,
A king might wish to hold in fee.

What doth the poor man's son inherit?
   A patience learned of being poor.
Courage, if sorrow come, to bear it,
   A fellow-feeling that is sure
   To make the outcast bless his door;
A heritage, it seems to me,
A king might wish to hold in fee.

O rich man's son! there is a toil,
   That with all others level stands;
Large charity doth never soil,
   But only whiten, soft white hands, —
   This is the best crop from thy lands;
A heritage, it seems to me,
Worth being rich to hold in fee.

O poor man's son! scorn not thy state;
   There is worse weariness than thine,
In merely being rich and great;
   Toil only gives the soul to shine,
   And makes rest fragrant and benign;
A heritage, it seems to me,
Worth being poor to hold in fee.

Both, heirs to some six feet of sod,
  Are equal in the earth at last;
Both, children of the same dear God,
  Prove title to your heirship vast
  By record of a well-filled past;
A heritage, it seems to me,
Well worth a life to hold in fee.

J. R. LOWELL.

PRIDE.

How proud we are! how fond to show
Our clothes, and call them rich and new;
When the poor sheep and silk-worm wore
That very clothing long before.

The tulip and the butterfly
Appear in gayer coats than I;
Let me be dressed fine as I will,
Flies, worms, and flowers exceed me still.

But let me seek and strive to find
Inward adorning of the mind;
Knowledge and virtue, truth and grace,
These are the robes of richest dress.

This never fades, it ne'er grows old,
Nor fears the rain, nor moth, nor mould;
It takes no spot, but still refines;
The more 't is worn, the more it shines.

In this on earth would I appear,
Then go to heaven and wear it there ;
God will approve it in his sight
'T is his own work, and his delight.

THE NOBLY BORN.

WHO counts himself as nobly born,
    Is noble in despite of place,
And honors are but bands to one
    Who wears them not with nature's grace.

The prince may sit with clown or churl,
    Nor feel his state disgraced thereby ;
But he who has but small esteem
    Husbands that little carefully.

Then, be thou peasant, be thou peer,
    Count it still more than art thine own ;
Stand on a larger heraldry
    Than that of nation or of zone.

What though not bid to knightly halls ?
    Those halls have missed a courtly guest ;
That mansion is not privileged,
    Which is not open to the best.

Give honor due when custom asks,
　　Nor wrangle for the lesser claim ;
It is not to be destitute,
　　To have the thing without the name.

Then, dost thou come of noble blood,
　　Disgrace not thy good company ;
If lowly born, so bear thyself
　　That gentle blood may come of thee.

Strive not with pain to scale the height
　　Of some fair garden's petty wall,
But scale the open mountain-side,
　　Whose summit rises over all.

DISCIPLES' HYMN-BOOK.

THE PEBBLE AND THE ACORN.

" I AM a Pebble, and yield to none ! "
Were swelling words of a tiny stone,
" Nor time nor season can alter me ;
I am abiding, while ages flee.
The pelting hail and the drizzling rain
Have tried to soften me long in vain ;
And the tender dew has sought to melt,
Or touch my heart ; but it was not felt.
There 's none that can tell about my birth,
For I 'm as old as the big, round earth.

The children of men arise, and pass
Out of the world like blades of grass;
And many a foot on me has trod,
That's gone from sight, and under the sod!
I am a Pebble! but who art thou,
Rattling along from the restless bough?"

The Acorn was shocked at the rude salute,
And lay for a moment abashed and mute;
She never before had been so near
This gravelly ball, the mundane sphere;
And she felt for a time at a loss to know
How to answer a thing so coarse and low.
But to give reproof of a nobler sort
Than the angry look, or the keen retort,
At length she said, in a gentle tone:
" Since it has happened that I am thrown
From the lighter element, where I grew,
Down to another, so hard and new,
And beside a personage so august,
Abased, I will cover my head with dust,
And quickly retire from the sight of one
Whom time, nor season, nor storm, nor sun,
Nor the gentle dew, nor the grinding heel
Has ever subdued, or made to feel!"
And soon, in the earth, she sunk away
From the comfortless spot where the Pebble lay.

But it was not long ere the soil was broke
By the peering head of an infant oak!

And, as it arose and its branches spread,
The Pebble looked up, and wondering said,
" A modest Acorn ! never to tell
What was enclosed in its simple shell ;
That the pride of the forest was folded up
In the narrow space of its little cup !
And meekly to sink in the darksome earth,
Which proves that nothing could hide her worth !
And oh ! how many will tread on me,
To come and admire the beautiful tree,
Whose head is towering towards the sky,
Above such a worthless thing as I !
Useless and vain, a cumberer here,
I have been idling from year to year.
But never, from this, shall a vaunting word
From the humbled Pebble again be heard,
Till something without me or within
Shall show the purpose for which I 've been !"
The Pebble its vow could not forget,
And it lies there wrapt in silence yet.

H. F. Gould.

LITTLE THINGS.

A SPIDER is a little thing,
But once a spider saved a king ;
The little bees are wiser far
Than buffalos and lions are ;

Little men may do much harm ;
Little girls may learn to charm ;
Little boys may shame their sires,
And little sparks become great fires ;
A little pen may write a word
By which a nation shall be stirred ;
A little money, wisely spent,
A world of sorrow may prevent ;
A little counsel, rightly given,
May lift a sinful soul to heaven.
Little losses, day by day,
Would waste old Rothschild's wealth away ;
A little needle in the eye
May cause an elephant to die ;
A little fault, if left to grow,
An emperor may overthrow ;
A little word, but spoke in jest,
May rob your neighbor of his rest ;
A little selfishness and pride
The kindest household may divide ;
Little vices many times
Out-Herod felonies and crimes ;
And little virtues in the sum
Great excellences do become.

MELODIES FOR CHILDHOOD.

THE KING'S EXAMPLE.

ONCE Sultan Nushirvan the just, hunting,
Stopped in an open field to take a lunch.
He wanted salt, and to a servant said,
" Go, get some at the nearest house, but pay
The price the peasant asks."   " Great king," exclaimed
The servant, " thou art lord o'er all this realm ;
Why take the pains to *buy* a little salt ? "
" It is a little thing," said Nushirvan,
" And so, at first, was all the evil whose
Most monstrous load now presses so the world.
Were there no little wrongs, no great could be.
If I from off a poor man's tree should pluck
A single apple, straight my slaves would rob
The whole tree to its roots : if I should seize
Five eggs, my ministers at once would snatch
A hundred hens.   Therefore strict justice must
I, even in unimportant acts, observe.
Bring salt, but pay the peasant what he asks."

ALGER'S ORIENTAL POETRY.

EACH CAN DO SOMETHING.

WHAT if the little rain should say,
  " So small a drop as I
Can ne'er refresh those thirsty fields ;
  I 'll tarry in the sky."

What if the shining beam of noon
  Should in its fountain stay,
Because its single light alone
  Cannot create a day.

Does not each rain-drop help to form
  The cool refreshing shower ?
And every ray of light to warm
  And beautify the flower ?

Then let each child its influence give,
  O Lord ! to truth and thee ;
So shall its power by all be felt,
  However small it be.

SOUTHERN CHURCHMAN.

EVERY LITTLE HELPS.

SUPPOSE a little twinkling star,
  Away in yonder sky,
Should say, what light can reach so far
  From such a star as I ?
Not many rays of mine so far
  As yonder earth can fall, —
The others so much brighter are,
  I will not shine at all !

Suppose a bright green leaf, that grows
  Upon the rosebush near,
Should say, because I 'm not a rose,
  I will not linger here ;
Or that a dew-drop, fresh and bright,
  Upon that fragrant flower,
Should say, I 'll vanish out of sight,
  Because I 'm not a shower !

Suppose a little child should say,
  Because I 'm not a man,
I will not try, in word or play,
  To do what good I can !
Dear child, each star *some* light can give,
  Though gleaming faintly there ;
Each rose-leaf helps the plant to live,
  Each dew-drop keeps it fair !

And our good Father who 's in heaven,
  And doth all creatures view,
To every little child has given
  Some needful work to do :
Kind deeds toward those with whom you live,
  Kind words and actions right,
Shall 'mid the world's worst darkness give
  A little precious light !

CHOICE POEMS.

LITTLE DEEDS.

NOT mighty deeds make up the sum
    Of happiness below,
But little acts of kindliness,
    Which any child may show.

A merry sound, to cheer the babe
    And tell a friend is near, —
A word of ready sympathy,
    To dry the childish tear, —

A glass of water timely brought, —
    An offered easy-chair, —
A turning of the window-blind,
    That all may feel the air, —

An early flower, unasked bestowed, —
    A light and cautious tread, —
A voice to gentlest whisper hushed,
    To spare the aching head, —

O, deeds like these, though little things,
    Yet purest love disclose,
As fragrant perfume on the air
    Reveals the hidden rose.

Our Heavenly Father loves to see
    These precious fruits of love ;
And, if we only serve him here,
    We 'll dwell with him above.

THE MOUNTAIN TORRENT.

FAIR streamlet running
  Where violets grow
Under the elm-trees,
  Murmuring low ;
Rippling gently
  Amid the grass ;
I have a fancy,
  As I pass ;
I have a fancy as I see
The trailing willows kissing thee ;
As I behold the daisies pied,
The harebells nodding at thy side ;
The sheep that feed upon thy brink,
The birds that stoop thy wave to drink ;
Thy blooms that tempt the bees to stray,
And all the life that tracks thy way.

I deem thou flowest
  Through grassy meads
To show the beauty
  Of gentle deeds ;
To show how happy
  The world might be,
If man, observant,
  Copied thee ;
To show how small a stream may pour
Verdure and beauty on either shore ;

To teach what humble men might do,
If their lives were pure, and their hearts were true;
And what a wealth they might dispense,
In modest, calm beneficence;
Marking their course, as thou dost thine,
By wayside flowers of love divine.

CHARLES MACKAY.

WHO IS MY NEIGHBOR?

THY neighbor? It is he whom thou
    Hast power to aid and bless,
Whose aching heart or burning brow
    Thy soothing hand may press.

Thy neighbor? 'T is the fainting poor,
    Whose eye with want is dim,
Whom hunger sends from door to door; —
    Go thou, and succor him.

Thy neighbor? 'T is that weary man,
    Whose years are at their brim,
Bent low with sickness, cares, and pain; —
    Go thou and comfort him.

Thy neighbor? 'T is the heart bereft
    Of every earthly gem;
Widow and orphan, helpless left; —
    Go thou and shelter them.

Thy neighbor ?   Yonder toiling slave,
   Fettered in thought and limb,
Whose hopes are all beyond the grave ; —
   Go thou and ransom him.

Whene'er thou meet'st a human form
   Less favored than thine own,
Remember 't is thy neighbor worm, —
   Thy mother, or thy son.

O, pass not, pass not heedless by ;
   Perhaps thou canst redeem
The breaking heart from misery ; —
   Go, share thy lot with him.

PEABODY.

THE LITTLE MATCH-SELLERS.

ARE all your matches sold, Tom ?
   Is all your selling done ?
Then let us to the flowery fields,
   To warm us in the sun.
To warm us in the sweet, sweet sun, —
   To feel his heavenly glow ;
For his kind looks are the only looks
   Of kindness that we know.

We 'll call the sun our father, Tom !
   We 'll call the sun our mother !

We 'll call each little charming beam
    A sister or a brother !
He thinks no shame to kiss us,
    Although we ragged go ;
For his kind looks are the only looks
    Of kindness that we know.

We 'll tell him all our sorrows, Tom !
    We 'll tell him all our care, —
We 'll tell him where we sleep at night,
    We 'll tell him how we fare ;
And then — O then ! — to cheer us,
    How sweetly he will glow ! —
For his kind looks are the only looks
    Of kindness that we know.

CHOICE POEMS.

FORGIVE THY BROTHER.

FORGIVE thy brother who has erred,
    And take him by the hand ;
And as you speak a generous word,
    Assist his feet to stand.

Joy 'll sparkle in his eye to hear
    Thy words of gentle tone ;
Forgiveness breathed upon his ear,
    And love and kindness shown,

Will make him rise to life again,
   And shun the path he trod,
When, in the round of Folly's train,
   He broke from Truth and God.

Forgive thy brother — even now
   A smile is on his cheek ;
The glow of heaven has tinged his brow, —
   Speak, and forgive him — speak !

THE BEGGAR'S REVENGE.

THE king's proud favorite at a beggar threw a stone :
He picked it up, as if it had for alms been thrown.

He bore it in his bosom long with bitter ache,
And sought his time revenge with that same stone to
   take.

One day he heard a street mob's hoarse commingled cry :
The favorite comes ! — but draws no more the admiring
   eye.

He rides an ass, from all his haughty state disgraced ;
And by the rabble's mocking gibes his way is traced.

The stone from out his bosom swift the beggar draws,
And, flinging it away, exclaims, " A fool I was ! "

'T is madness to attack, when in his power, your foe,
And meanness then to strike when he has fallen low.

                                    ALGER'S ORIENTAL POETRY.

SPEAK GENTLY.

SPEAK gently ! it is better far
  To rule by love than fear ;
Speak gently ! let not harsh words mar
  The good we might do here.

Speak gently to the aged one ;
  Grieve not the care-worn heart ;
The sands of life are nearly run :
  Let such in peace depart.

Speak gently, kindly, to the poor,
  Let no harsh tone be heard ;
They have enough they must endure
  Without an unkind word !

Speak gently ! He who gave his life,
  To bend man's stubborn will,
When elements were in fierce strife,
  Said to them, " Peace, be still ! "

Speak gently ! 't is a little thing,
  Dropped in the heart's deep well,
The good, the joy, which it may bring,
  Eternity shall tell.

N O.

THERE 's a word very short, but decided and plain,
   And speaks to the purpose at once ;
Not a child but its meaning can quickly explain,
   Yet oft 't is too hard to pronounce :
What a world of vexation and trouble 't would spare,
   What pleasure and peace 't would bestow,
If we turned, when temptation would lure and ensnare,
   And firmly repulsed it with " No ! "

When the idler would tempt us, with trifles and play,
   To waste the bright moments so dear ;
When the scoffer unholy our faith would gainsay,
   And mock at the word we revere ;
When deception and falsehood and guile would invite,
   And fleeting enjoyments bestow,
Never palter with truth for a transient delight,
   But check the first impulse with " No ! "

In the morning of life, in maturity's day,
   Whatever the cares that engage,
Be the precepts of virtue our guide and our stay,
   Our solace from youth unto age !
Thus the heart shall ne'er waver, no matter how tried,
   But firmness and constancy show,
And when passion or folly would draw us aside,
   We 'd spurn the seducer with " No ! "

GEORGE BENNETT.

THE FORSAKEN.

O THOU whose brow, serene and calm,
   From earthly stain is free,
View not with scorn that lost one's fate,
   — She once was pure like thee.

Though in thy lovely form and face
   Health's rosy glow we see,
Yet shrink not from that faded form
   — She once was fair like thee !

Thou in thy father's home may dwell
   In peace and purity ;
Yet pity her, though friendless now,
   — She once was blest like thee.

Perchance the smiles of love are thine,
   Its joyful ecstasy ;
Then weep for that forsaken one,
   — She once was loved like thee.

And still, 'mid shame, and guilt, and woe.
   One Being loves her still !
Who makes thee blest, and pours on her
   The world's extremest ill.

He knows the secret lure that led
   Her youthful steps astray ;

He knows that thou, in all thy pride,
   Might fall from him away;

Then, with the love of Him who said,
   " Depart, and sin no more,"
Shield from despair that wretched one,
   And bid her pangs be o'er.

SACRED OFFERING.

THE FAIRY'S GIFT.

O DID you not hear in your nursery
   The tale that gossips tell,
Of two young girls that came to drink
   At a certain fairy well?

The words of the younger were as sweet
   As the smile of her ruby lip;
But the tongue of the eldest seemed to move
   As if venom were on its tip.

At the well a beggar accosted them,
   (A sprite, in mean disguise,)
The eldest spake with a scornful brow,
   The younger with tear-dimmed eyes.

Cried the fairy, " Whenever you speak, sweet girl,
   Pure gems from your lips shall fall;

11 *

But whenever *you* utter a word, proud maid,
   From your tongue shall a serpent crawl!"

And have you not met with these sisters oft,
   In the haunts of the old and young?
The first with her pure, unsullied lip,
   The last with her serpent tongue?

The first is GOOD NATURE. Diamonds bright
   O'er the darkest theme she throws;
The last is SLANDER — leaving the blight
   Of the snake, wherever she goes.

DON'T FRET.

HAS a neighbor injured you?
               Don't fret:
You will yet come off the best;
   He 's the most to answer for,
Never mind it, let it rest.
               Don't fret:

Has a wicked lie been told?
               Don't fret:
It will run itself to death,
   If you let it quite alone,
It will die for want of breath;
               Don't fret.

Are your enemies at work?
                    Don't fret:
They can't injure you a whit;
    If they find you heed them not,
They will soon be glad to quit;
                    Don't fret.

Is adversity your lot?
                    Don't fret:
Fortune's wheel keeps turning round,
    Every spoke will reach the top,
Which, like you, is going down;
                    Don't fret.

THANKFULNESS.

SOME murmur when their sky is clear
    And wholly bright to view,
If one small speck of dark appear
    In their great heaven of blue;
And some with thankful love are filled,
    If but one streak of light,
One ray of God's great mercy gild
    The darkness of their night.

In palaces are hearts that ask,
    In discontent and pride,

Why life is such a weary task,
    And all good things denied ;
And hearts in poorest huts admire
    How love has in their aid
(Love that not ever seems to tire)
    Such rich provision made.

O HUMBLY take what God bestows,
    And, like his own fair flowers,
Look up in sunshine with a smile,
    And gently bend in showers.

HOPE.

THE night is mother of the day,
    The winter of the spring,
And ever upon old decay
    The greenest mosses cling.

Behind the cloud the starlight lurks ;
    Through showers the sunbeams fall ;
For God, who loveth all his works,
    Has left his hope with all.

                              J. G. WHITTIER.

TWO WAYS.

THERE are two ways to live on earth, —
    Two ways to judge, — to act, — to view ;
For all things here have double birth, —
    A right and wrong, — a false and true !

Some beings, wheresoe'er they go,
    Find naught to please or to exalt, —
Their constant study but to show
    Perpetual modes of finding fault.

While others, in the ceaseless round
    Of daily wants, and daily care,
Can yet cull flowers from common ground,
    And twice enjoy the joy they share !

O, happy they who happy *make*, —
    Who, blessing, still themselves are blest !
Who something spare for others' sake,
    And strive, in all things, for the best !

CHARLES SWAIN.

NEVER RAIL AT THE WORLD.

NEVER rail at the world — it is just as we make it :
    We see not the flower, if we set not the seed ;
And as for ill-luck, why, it 's just as we take it, —
    The heart that 's in earnest no bars can impede.

You question the justice which governs man's breast,
  And say that the search for true friendship is vain ;
But remember, this world, though it be not the best,
  Is the next to the best we shall ever attain.

IBID.

IN SICKNESS.

WHEN upon the bed of languor
    Weak and feverish we toss;
Should something like impatient anger
    Come the weary mind across,
        The only remedy that's found
            To drive away the sin,
        Is gentle words to those around,
            And holy thoughts within.

Thus, in prison hours full often,
    Saints their rugged beds could smooth ;
Thus their stern jailer's heart could soften,
    And their own sad bosoms soothe.
        How did Joseph, dungeon-bound,
            Release and honor win ?
        By gentle words to those around,
            And holy thoughts within.

Then, although a prisoner lying
    Chained in weariness and pain,

My soul through tedious hours is sighing
For sunshine, and for health again ;
    Yet in my chamber ne'er be found
      A dream of selfish sin,
But gentle words to those around,
    And holy thoughts within.

REV. W. CALVERT.

THE CRIPPLE.

I 'M a helpless, crippled child ;
    Gentle Christians, pity me ;
Once in rosy health I smiled,
    Blythe and gay as you can be,
And, upon the village green
First in every sport was seen.

Now, alas! I 'm weak and low,
    Cannot either work or play ;
Tottering on my crutches slow,
    Drag along my weary way ;
Now no longer dance or sing
Gayly in the merry ring.

Many sleepless nights I live,
    Turning on my weary bed :
Softest pillows cannot give
    Slumber to my aching head ;

Constant anguish makes it fly
From my wakeful, heavy eye.

And when morning beams return,
  Still no comfort beams for me ;
Still my limbs with fever burn,
  Painful shoots my crippled knee,
And another tedious day
Passes slow and sad away.

From my chamber-windows high,
  Lifted to my easy-chair,
I the village green can spy —
  Once I used to follow there,
March, or beat my new-bought drum :
Happy times ! no more to come.

There I see my fellows gay
  Sporting on the daisied turf,
And, amidst their cheerful play,
  Stopped by many a merry laugh ;
But the sight I cannot bear,
Leaning in my easy-chair.

Let not then the scoffing eye
  Laugh my twisted leg to see ;
Gentle Christian, passing by,
  Stop awhile, and pity me,
And for you I 'll breathe a prayer,
Leaning on my easy-chair.

THE BOY AND THE FLOWER.

FROM THE DANISH OF HANS ANDERSEN.

An angel is bearing to heaven the spirit of a girl, and carries with him a rose. The newly cleansed soul asks the meaning of it. The angel answers:—

" In the city we are leaving
  There lay a dying boy ;
The bud I bear to heaven
  It was his only joy.

" His days were long and dreary,
  In the dismal, dismal street,
And at night 't was very dreary
  To count the passing feet.

" For he lay from morn to midnight
  Watching the shadows pass,
And never saw the sunlight,
  Nor the pleasant country grass.

" But when his flower opened
  He knew the fields were green,
And its falling leaves betokened
  That all the flowers had been.

" He saw it ere he slumbered,
  He watched it as it grew ;

Q

Its very leaves he numbered,
   And its coming bud he knew.

" And to his aching bosom
   It brought such happy rest,
That he loved his little blossom
   Next to his mother — best.

" 'T was in the white December
   God took the boy above ;
Yet doth he still remember
   His lowly flower-love.

" It was not made to wither,
   A thing so good and fair ;
Therefore I sought it thither,
   And take it to him there.

" In Heaven's soil abiding,
   These buds shall brighter blow,
And tell us pleasant tiding
   Of those that live below.

" How know'st thou this, bright Power ? "
   Then splendidly he smiled :
" Should I not know *my* flower ? —
   I was that sickly child ! "

TRANS. BY MR. E. ARNOLD.

CŒUR DE LION AT THE BIER OF HIS FATHER.

TORCHES were blazing clear,
　　Hymns pealing deep and slow,
Where a king lay stately on his bier
　　In the church of Fontivraud.
Banners of battle o'er him hung,
　　And warriors slept beneath,
And light, as noon's broad light, was flung
　　On the settled face of death.

On the settled face of death
　　A strong and ruddy glare ;
Though dimmed at times by the censer's breath,
　　Yet it still fell brightest there :
As if each deeply furrowed trace
　　Of earthly years to show, —
Alas ! that sceptred mortal's race
　　Had surely closed in woe !

The marble floor was swept
　　By many a long, dark stole,
As the kneeling priests round him that slept
　　Sang mass for the parted soul ;
And solemn were the strains they poured
　　Through the stillness of the night,
With the cross above, and the crown and sword,
　　And the silent king in sight.

There was heard a heavy clang
As of steel-girt men the tread,
And the tombs, and the hollow pavement rang
With a sounding thrill of dread ;
And the holy chant was hushed awhile,
As, by the torch's flame,
A gleam of arms, up the sweeping aisle,
With a mail-clad leader came.

He came with haughty look,
An eagle glance and clear,
But his proud heart through his breastplate shook,
When he stood beside the bier !
He stood there still with drooping brow,
And clasped hands o'er it raised ; —
For his father lay before him low ; —
It was Cœur de Lion gazed !

And silently he strove
With the workings in his breast ;
But there 's more in late-repentant love
Than steel can keep suppressed !
And his tears broke forth, at last, like rain ; —
Men held their breath in awe,
For his face was seen by his warrior-train,
And he recked not that they saw.

He looked upon the dead,
And sorrow seemed to lie,

A weight of sorrow even like lead,
　　Pale on the fast-shut eye.
He stooped, and kissed the frozen cheek,
　　And the heavy hand of clay,
Till bursting words, yet all too weak,
　　Gave his soul's passion way.

" O father ! is it vain,
　　This late remorse and deep ?
Speak to me, father, once again :
　　I weep, — behold, I weep !
Alas ! my guilty pride and ire !
　　Were but this work undone,
I would give England's crown, my sire,
　　To have thee bless thy son !

" Speak to me ! mighty grief,
　　Ere now the dust hath stirred !
Hear me ! but hear me, father, chief !
　　My king ! I must be heard.
Hushed, hushed ; — how is it that I call,
　　And that thou answerest not ?
When was it thus ? — woe, woe for all
　　The love my soul forgot !

" Thy silver hairs I see,
　　So still, so sadly bright !
And, father ! father ! but for me
　　They had not been so white !
I bore thee down, high heart ! at last,
　　No longer couldst thou strive ;

O, for one moment of the past
    To kneel and say, ' Forgive ! '

" Thou wert the noblest king
    On royal throne e'er seen ;
And thou didst wear, in knightly ring,
    Of all the stateliest mien ;
And thou didst prove, where spears are proved
    In war, the bravest heart —
O, ever the renowned and loved
    Thou wert ; — and there thou art !

" Thou, that my boyhood's guide
    Didst take fond joy to be ! —
The times I 've sported by thy side,
    And climbed the parent-knee !
And there before the blessed shrine,
    My sire ! I see thee lie ;
How will that still, sad face of thine
    Look on me till I die ! "

MRS. HEMANS.

THE OLD FOLKS' ROOM.

THE old man sat by the chimney-side —
    His face was wrinkled and wan,
And he leaned both hands on his stout oak cane,
    As if all his work were done.

His coat was of good old-fashioned gray,
  The pockets were deep and wide,
Where his " specks " and his steel tobacco-box,
  Lay snugly side by side.

The old man liked to stir the fire,
  So, near him the tongs were kept ;
Sometimes he mused as he gazed at the coals,
  Sometimes he sat and slept.

What saw he in the embers there ?
  Ah ! pictures of other years ;
And now and then they wakened smiles,
  But oftener started tears.

His good wife sat on the other side,
  In a high-backed, flag-seat chair ;
I see 'neath the pile of her muslin cap
  The sheen of her silvery hair.

There 's a happy look on her aged face,
  As she busily knits for him,
And Nellie takes up the stitches dropped,
  For grandmother's eyes are dim.

Their children come and read the news,
  To pass the time each day ;
How it stirs the blood in an old man's heart,
  To hear of the world away.

'T is a homely scene, I told you so,
　　But pleasant it is to view;
At least I thought it so myself,
　　And sketched it down for you.

Be kind unto the old, my friend,
　　They 're worn with this world's strife,
Though bravely once perchance they fought
　　The stern, fierce battle of life.

They taught our youthful feet to climb
　　Upward life's rugged steep;
Then let us gently lead them down
　　To where the weary sleep.

GOOD FROM EVIL.

THE clouds which rise with thunder, slake
　　Our thirsty souls with rain;
The blow most dreaded falls to break
　　From off our limbs a chain;
And wrongs of man to man but make
　　The love of God more plain.
As through the shadowy lens of even
The eye looks farthest into heaven,
On gleams of star and depths of blue
The glaring sunshine never knew!

J. G. WHITTIER.

BEAUTY AND DUTY.

I SLEPT — and dreamed that life was beauty;
I woke — and found that life was duty.
Was my dream, then, a shadowy lie?
Toil on, sad heart, courageously;
And thou shalt find thy dream shall be
A noonday light and truth to thee.

LUCY HOOPER.

EXCELSIOR.

THE shades of night were falling fast,
As through an Alpine village passed
A youth, who bore 'mid snow and ice,
A banner with the strange device,
    Excelsior!

His brow was sad; his eye beneath,
Flashed like a falchion from its sheath,
And like a silver clarion rung
The accents of that unknown tongue,
    Excelsior!

In happy homes he saw the light
Of household fires gleam warm and bright;

12

Above, the spectral glaciers shone,
And from his lips escaped a groan,
Excelsior!

" Try not the Pass!" the old man said;
" Dark lowers the tempest overhead,
The roaring torrent is deep and wide!"
And loud that clarion voice replied,
Excelsior!

" O stay," the maiden said, " and rest
Thy weary head upon this breast!"
A tear stood in his bright blue eye,
But still he answered with a sigh,
Excelsior!

" Beware the pine-tree's withered branch!
Beware the fearful avalanche!"
This was the peasant's last good-night;
A voice replied, far up the height,
Excelsior!

At break of day, as heavenward
The pious monks of Saint Bernard
Uttered the oft-repeated prayer,
A voice cried through the startled air,
Excelsior!

A traveller, by the faithful hound,
Half buried in the snow was found,

Still grasping in his hand of ice
That banner with the strange device,
    Excelsior!

There in the twilight cold and gray,
Lifeless, but beautiful, he lay,
And from the sky, serene and far,
A voice fell, like a falling star,
    Excelsior!

LONGFELLOW.

A FAREWELL.

MY fairest child, I have no song to give you;
  No lark could pipe to skies so dull and gray:
Yet, ere we part, one lesson I can leave you
    For every day.

Be good, sweet maid, and let who will be clever;
  Do noble things, not dream them, all day long;
And so make life, death, and that vast Forever
    One grand, sweet song.

CHARLES KINGSLEY.

PART VI.

THE END.

DEATH OF THE NEWLY BAPTIZED.

LYRA INNOCENTIUM.

WHAT purer, brighter sight on earth, than when
   The sun looks down upon a drop of dew,
Hid in some nook from all but angels' ken,
    And with his radiance bathes it through and through,
    Then into realms too clear for our frail view

Exhales and draws it with absorbing love ?
  And what if Heaven therein give token true
Of grace that new-born dying infants prove,
Just touched with Jesus' light, then lost in joys above ?

KEBLE.

LITTLE BESSIE.

" Hug me closer, closer, mother ;
Put your arms around me tight ;
I am cold and tired, mother,
And I feel so strange to-night !
Something hurts me here, dear mother,
Like a stone upon my breast :
O, I wonder, wonder, mother,
Why it is I cannot rest !

" All the day, while you were working,
As I lay upon my bed,
I was trying to be patient,
And to think of what you said :
How the kind and blessed Jesus
Loves his lambs to watch and keep ;
And I wished he 'd come and take me
In his arms, that I might sleep.

" Just before the lamp was lighted,
Just before the children came,

While the room was very quiet,
I heard some one call my name.
All at once the windows opened:
In a field were lambs and sheep;
Some from out a brook were drinking,
Some were lying fast asleep.

" But I could not see the Saviour,
Though I strained my eyes to see;
And I wondered, if he saw me,
If he 'd speak to such as me.
In a moment I was looking
On a world so bright and fair,
Which was full of little children,
And they seemed so happy there.

" They were singing, O how sweetly!
Sweeter songs I never heard;
They were singing sweeter, mother,
. Than can sing our pretty bird;
And while I my breath was holding,
One so bright upon me smiled,
That I knew it must be Jesus,
And he said, ' Come here, my child;

" ' Come up here, my little Bessie;
Come up here, and live with me;
Where the children never suffer,
But are happier than you see.'
Then I thought of all you told me

R

Of that bright and happy land :
I was going, when you called me,
When you came and kissed my hand.

" And at first I felt so sorry
You had called me : I would go —
O, to sleep, and never suffer ! —
Mother, don't be crying so !
Hug me closer, closer, mother ;
Put your arms around me tight ;
O, how much I love you, mother !
But I feel so strange to-night ! "

And the mother pressed her closer
To her overburdened breast ;
On the heart so near to breaking
Lay the heart so near at rest !
In the solemn hour of midnight,
In the darkness calm and deep,
Lying on her mother's bosom,
Little Bessie fell asleep !

MELODIES FOR CHILDHOOD.

THE LOST LITTLE ONE.

THE fairy form our home that blest
  With sport and prattle gay,
The little one we loved the best
  From earth has passed away.

We miss her footfall on the floor,
 Amidst the nursery din,
Her tip-tap at our bedroom door,
 Her bright face peeping in.

And when to Heaven's high courts above
 Ascends our social prayer,
Though there are voices that we love,
 One sweet voice is not there.

And dreary seem the hours, and lone,
 That drag themselves along,
Now from our board her smile is gone,
 And from our hearth her song.

We miss that farewell laugh of hers,
 With its light, joyous sound,
And the kiss between the balusters,
 When good-night time comes round.

And empty is her little bed,
 And on her pillow there
Must never rest that cherub head
 With its soft silken hair.

But often, as we wake and weep,
 Our midnight thoughts will roam,
To visit her cold, dreamless sleep,
 In her last narrow home.

Then, then it is Faith's tear-dimmed eyes
   See through ethereal space,
Amidst the angel-crowded skies,
   That dear, that well-known face.

With beckoning hand she seems to say,
   "Though, all her sufferings o'er,
'Your little one is borne away
   To this celestial shore,

"Doubt not she longs to welcome you
   To her glad, bright abode,
There, happy, endless ages through,
   To live with her and God."

Rev. W. Calvert.

RESIGNATION.

There is no flock, however watched and tended,
   But one dead lamb is there !
There is no fireside, howsoe'er defended,
   But has one vacant chair !

The air is full of farewells to the dying,
   And mournings for the dead ;
The heart of Rachel for her children crying
   Will not be comforted !

Let us be patient! these severe afflictions
   Not from the ground arise,
But oftentimes celestial benedictions
   Assume this dark disguise.

We see but dimly through the mists and vapors;
   Amid these earthly damps
What seem to us but dim, funereal tapers
   May be Heaven's distant lamps.

There is no Death! what seems so is transition;
   This life of mortal breath
Is but a suburb of the life elysian,
   Whose portal we call Death.

She is not dead — the child of our affection —
   But gone unto that school,
Where she no longer needs our poor protection,
   And Christ himself doth rule.

In that great cloister's stillness and seclusion,
   By guardian angels led,
Safe from temptation, safe from sin's pollution,
   She lives — whom we call dead.

Day after day we think what she is doing
   In those bright realms of air;
Year after year her tender steps pursuing,
   Behold her grown more fair.

Thus do we walk with her, and keep unbroken
   The bond which nature gives,
Thinking that our remembrance, though unspoken,
   May reach her where she lives.

Not as a child shall we again behold her;
   For when with raptures wild
In our embraces we again enfold her,
   She will not be a child;

But a fair maiden, in her Father's mansion,
   Clothed with celestial grace;
And beautiful with all the soul's expansion
   Shall we behold her face.

And though at times, impetuous with emotion
   And anguish long suppressed,
The swelling heart heaves moaning like the ocean
   That cannot be at rest;

We will be patient! and assuage the feeling
   We cannot wholly stay;
By silence sanctifying, not concealing,
   The grief that must have way.

LONGFELLOW.

THE ALPINE SHEPHERD.

WHEN on my ear your loss was knelled.
  And tender sympathy upburst,
A little rill from memory swelled,
  Which once had soothed my bitter thirst.

And I was fain to bear to you
  Some portion of their mild relief,
That it might be as healing dew,
  To steal some fever from your grief.

After our child's untroubled breath
  Up to the Father took its way,
And on our home the shade of death
  Like a long twilight haunting lay;

And friends came round with us to weep
  Her little spirit's swift remove,
This story of the Alpine sheep
  Was told to us by one we love:

" They in the valley's sheltering care
  Soon crop the meadow's tender prime,
And when the sod grows brown and bare,
  The shepherd strives to make them climb

" To airy shelves of pasture green,
    That hang along the mountain's side,
Where grass and flowers together lean,
    And down through mist the sunbeams slide.

" But naught can tempt the timid things
    The steep and rugged path to try,
Though sweet the shepherd calls and sings,
    And seared below the pastures lie,

" Till in his arms the lambs he takes,
    Along the dizzy verge to go,
Then, heedless of the rifts and breaks,
    They follow on o'er rock and snow.

" And in those pastures lifted fair,
    More dewy soft than lowland mead,
The shepherd drops his tender care,
    And sheep and lambs together feed."

This parable, by Nature breathed,
    Blew on me as the south-wind free
O'er frozen brooks, that float unsheathed
    From icy thraldom to the sea.

A blissful vision through the night
    Would all my happy senses sway,
Of the Good Shepherd on the height,
    Or climbing up the starry way,

Holding our little lamb asleep,
  And like the burden of the sea
Sounded that voice along the deep,
  Saying, " Arise, and follow me ! "

MARIA LOWELL.

GOING HOME.

" Suffer little children to come unto me, and forbid them not; for of such is
the kingdom of Heaven."

THEY are going — only going —
  Jesus called them long ago ;
All the wintry time they 're passing
  Softly as the falling snow.
When the violets in the spring-time
  Catch the azure of the sky,
They are carried out to slumber
  Sweetly where the violets lie.

They are going — only going —
  When with summer earth is dressed,
In their cold hands holding roses
  Folded to each silent breast ;
When the autumn hangs red banners
  Out above the harvest sheaves,
They are going — ever going —
  Thick and fast, like falling leaves.

All along the mighty ages,
　　All adown the solemn time,
They have taken up their homeward
　　March to that serener clime,
Where the watching, waiting angels
　　Lead them from the shadow dim,
To the brightness of His presence
　　Who has called them unto him.

They are going — only going —
　　Out of pain and into bliss —
Out of sad and sinful weakness
　　Into perfect holiness.
Snowy brows — no care shall shade them ;
　　Bright eyes — tears shall never dim ;
Rosy lips — no time shall fade them ;
　　Jesus called them unto him.

Little hearts forever stainless, —
　　Little hands as pure as they, —
Little feet by angels guided
　　Never a forbidden way !
They are going — ever going —
　　Leaving many a lonely spot ;
But 't is Jesus who has called them —
　　Suffer and forbid them not.

"OF SUCH IS THE KINGDOM OF HEAVEN."

O, WHY should children fear,
   When sickness dims the eye,
To lie down in the grave,
   And innocently die ;
Since Jesus Christ his word has given,
That such as these shall enter Heaven ?

Then weep not, parents dear,
   Because we go above ;
We leave you here below,
   To seek a tenderer love ;
For Jesus Christ his word has given,
That such as WE shall enter Heaven.

Sigh not o'er our pale brows,
   Where death has set his seal ;
Nor shrink at those chill hands,
   That have not power to feel,
For Jesus Christ his word has given,
That such as WE shall enter Heaven.

Let our young playmates come,
   And view the grassy mound,
And plant their early flowers
   As if 't were happy ground ;
For Jesus Christ his word has given,
That such as THEY shall enter Heaven.

MRS. GILMAN.

LITTLE PILGRIMS.

" WHO are they, whose little feet,
  Pacing life's dark journey through,
Now have reached that heavenly seat
  They had ever kept in view ? "
" I from Greenland's frozen land ; "
  " I from India's sultry plain ; "
" I from Afric's barren sand ; "
  " I from islands of the main."

All our earthly journey past,
  Every tear and pain gone by,
Here together meet at last,
  At the portals of the sky ;
Each the welcome " Come ! " awaits,
  Conquerors o'er death and sin !
Lift your heads, ye golden gates !
  And let the little travellers in.

J. EDMESTON.

CHILDREN'S PRAISES.

AROUND the throne of God in heaven
  Thousands of children stand, —
Children whose sins are all forgiven,
  A holy, happy band, —
    Singing, Glory, glory !

In flowing robes of spotless white
   See every one arrayed,
Dwelling in everlasting light,
   And joys that never fade, —
     Singing, Glory, glory!

Once they were little things like you,
   And lived on earth below,
And could not praise, as now they do,
   The Lord who loved them so, —
     Singing, Glory, glory!

What brought them to that world above,
   That heaven so bright and fair,
Where all is peace, and joy, and love:
   How come these children there, —
     Singing, Glory, glory?

On earth they sought the Saviour's grace,
   On earth they loved his name;
So now they see his blessed face,
   And stand before the Lamb, —
     Singing, Glory, glory!

THE SICK CHILD.

SEND down thy wingéd angel, God!
    Amidst this night so wild,
And bid him come where now we watch,
    And breathe upon our child!

She lies upon her pillow, pale,
    And moans within her sleep,
Or wakeneth with a patient smile,
    And striveth not to weep!

How gentle and how good a child
    She is, we know too well;
And dearer to her parents' hearts
    Than our weak words can tell.

We love, — we watch throughout the night,
    To aid, where need may be;
We hope, — and have despaired at times;
    But now we turn to Thee!

Send down thy sweet-souled angel, God!
    Amidst the darkness wild,
And bid him soothe our souls to-night,
    And heal our gentle child!

                            BARRY CORNWALL.

A MOTHER'S RECOMPENSE.

WHAT can a mother's heart repay,
      In after years,
For watchful night and weary day
Beside the cradle passed away,
      And anxious tears ?
To see her dear one tread the earth
In life and health, and childish mirth.

What can a mother's heart repay
      For later care, —
For words that heavenward point the way,
For counsel against passion's sway,
      And earnest prayer ?
To watch her little pilgrims press
Along the road to holiness.

This will a mother's heart repay,
      If that loved band,
Amidst life's doubtful battle-fray,
By grace sustained, shall often say,
      " Next to God's hand,
All of true happiness we know,
Mother, to thy dear self we owe."

                    REV. W. CALVERT.